NOBODY BUT YOU

A Callaway Wedding Novella

BARBARA FREETHY

NOBODY BUT YOU
© Copyright 2013 Barbara Freethy
ALL RIGHTS RESERVED

For information contact: barbara@barbarafreethy.com
Follow Barbara on Facebook:
www.facebook.com/barbarafreethybooks

NOBODY BUT YOU

A Callaway Wedding Novella

BARBARA FREETHY

Chapter One

"You're a beautiful bride, Emma," Nicole Callaway said, smiling at her sister in the full-length mirror.

Emma stared at herself in bemusement. This woman in the lacy white wedding dress wasn't her, was it? She was a tomboy turned firefighter turned arson investigator. She spent her days in coveralls and fire suits. She was lucky if she remembered to run a brush through her blonde hair, much less put on makeup, but today her sisters, Nicole and Shayla, had done her hair and forced her to wear eyeliner and lipstick. She barely recognized herself, but she was impressed.

"Damn, I look good," she said.

"Like a princess in a fairytale," Shayla said with a wistful sigh.

Emma turned around to give her youngest sister a smile. At twenty-four, Shayla was the baby of the Callaway family, and while on most days she was a pragmatic, logical, and rather brilliant medical student, today she was obviously caught up in bridal fantasies.

"Princess?" Emma challenged. "I look good enough to

be the queen."

"Always so ambitious," Nicole teased.

"I can't help it. I like to be on top."

Nicole laughed. "And how does Max feel about that?"

"I wasn't talking about *that*," she said. "Although, now that you mention it…"

"We don't need any more information," Nicole said quickly.

"I wasn't going to give you any," she replied. "And I've had to be ambitious. I'm a woman in a man's profession. If I don't fight, I'm done."

"I know," Nicole said with an understanding nod. "And it's not just doing the job well that motivates you, it's Dad's respect."

That was true. Jack Callaway's respect had been a driving force behind many of her ambitions, which was probably true for most of her siblings. Her father had a big personality and demanded achievement from everyone around him, his coworkers and his family members. But for her, his opinion was even more important, because Jack was second in charge of the San Francisco Fire Department, which technically made him her boss.

"It's different for me than for you," she said. "I work in Dad's world, and I can't let him down. I have to continually prove I'm as good as the boys."

"You've already proven that a dozen times over," Nicole said. "And today you're not a firefighter, you're a bride. This is your night, Em. You're the star, and the only one you have to share the spotlight with is Max. I don't think he'll steal your thunder."

"I don't know about that. He's going to look hot in that black tuxedo I forced him to rent," Emma said with a grin.

"I'm sure you're right, but everyone will still be looking at you," Nicole said with a smile. "If for no other reason than this may be the only time they see you in a long dress."

She tipped her head. "Good point." Her gaze moved to the clock on the bedside table. It was half past four, and the wedding ceremony was scheduled for six at a beautiful church in the presidio, followed by a reception at the San Francisco Yacht Club. "We should get going, don't you think?"

"I'll check on the limo," Shayla said. "It's supposed to be here now." On her way out of the bedroom, she paused in the doorway. "In case I don't get a chance to say it before the wedding, I'm really happy for you, Em, and I'm even happier that you got us bridesmaid dresses that aren't hideous. Thank you for that."

Emma smiled, thinking how pretty Shayla looked in the gold cocktail dress. She'd wanted a color to fit her holiday wedding, and what could be better than dresses the color of champagne? "I'm glad you like it." After Shayla left, Emma turned back to Nicole. "This whole day feels surreal. Here we are, standing in the bedroom we shared when we were teenagers, when we used to dream about the guy we were going to marry. Remember all the talks we used to have after we turned the lights out?"

"I do," Nicole said with a soft smile. "We were so worried we wouldn't find the right guys, but we did. I have Ryan, and you have Max. Life is good."

"Almost too good. I feel a little nervous, like this kind of happiness can't possibly last. It's silly to feel that way— isn't it?"

"Yes," Nicole said firmly. "That's just nerves talking, Emma. Love can last forever. Look at our grandparents. And look at Mom and Jack."

"But Mom's first marriage with our dad didn't work out. I'm sure she thought it would. How does anyone really know?"

"You don't know. You have to trust your feelings. Sometimes marriage takes work. Ryan and I have certainly had our challenges. But I believe that real love triumphs in the end." She paused. "Ryan and I lost our way for a while, but when Brandon was kidnapped, all the stupid stuff seemed so unimportant. I never want to lose my perspective like that again."

"Well, you're back together now."

"Stronger than ever," Nicole said with a nod, then she frowned. "You're not really having doubts about marrying Max, are you?"

She quickly shook her head. "No, I'm just jittery, and I don't know why. Max is wonderful."

"And he's the perfect man for you. He's smart and strong, and he'll always protect you and love you, even when you don't want protection and you're being a little too annoying to love," she teased.

Emma made a face at her. "Thanks for that."

"Seriously, stop worrying and enjoy the moment."

"You're right. I'm just nervous because this day has taken so long to get here." She had originally planned to marry Max in August, in a double wedding with her best friend, Sara, who, at the time, was engaged to her brother, Aiden. But Sara had gotten pregnant and needed to move up her wedding day. Emma had been forced to cancel the double wedding venue, which she couldn't afford on her own, and had rescheduled her wedding for two weeks before Christmas.

Now that December had arrived, she was happy with her new date. She loved winter—cold foggy mornings, the drizzle of rain on the window, and the holiday lights that turned ordinary streets into winter wonderlands. This time of the year felt magical, and so did her love for Max.

She hadn't liked him much at first. She'd met him on the job. She'd been working on an arson case, and he'd been the detective assigned to the homicide that resulted from the arson. She'd found him cocky and annoying and very territorial. It had soon become clear, however, that the sparks between them were not just the result of anger or irritation but also attraction.

She'd fought against that attraction, because she'd just gotten out of a bad relationship and wasn't eager to start another. And Max had been wary, too. He'd lived through his parents' bitter divorce and wasn't a big believer in marriage. But in the end, the love between them had been too strong to resist.

They'd fallen hard for each other, and their relationship had become the best possible mix of passion, friendship and respect. Max accepted her for who she was. And she did the same for him. It was the most honest relationship of her life, and today they would make an official and public commitment to each other. She couldn't wait.

"It may seem like the last few months have been really long to you, Emma," Nicole said. "But I think the year has flown by. So much has happened in our family. You and Max fell in love, Aiden and Sara had a baby girl, Drew fell for Ria and is now helping her parent her seventeen-year-old niece. It's been crazy!"

"Don't forget you found Brandon's twin brother, Kyle."

"And we met Kyle's mother, Jessica, who is already starting to feel like a sister," Nicole said with a nod. "We've had a lot of blessings this year."

Emma saw the moisture in her sister's eyes and felt a little teary herself. "Stop already. You're going to make me cry, and I know you don't want to have to do my makeup again."

Nicole laughed. "Very true. Okay, let's talk about a more practical matter."

"What's that?"

"I am so touched that you and Max want to include Brandon and Kyle in your ceremony, but I'm worried about Brandon being one of the ring bearers."

"Brandon and Kyle did fine at the rehearsal last night," Emma reminded her, understanding the concern in Nicole's eyes. Six-year-old Brandon was autistic, but since being reunited with his twin brother, Kyle, Brandon was showing marked improvement when it came to interacting with others, and she thought he could handle the ceremony. "Kyle will be there to help him," she added. "Besides, they're not going to carry the actual rings. Even if they bolt down the aisle or drop the pillows, it will still be fine."

"I just don't want anything to mar your perfect night. I can never predict what Brandon is going to do or what might spook him. He could freeze in the middle of the aisle and start screaming. Or he could run out of the church."

"Don't worry about it, Nicole. Jessica said she'd stand at the back in case Brandon decides to take off. She'll make sure he's okay. You said she's really good with him."

Nicole nodded, but there was still a little doubt in her eyes. "Brandon does like Jessica, or at least he tolerates her. The fact that Kyle loves her seems to carry some weight with him."

"It's going to be fine. And whatever Brandon does is not going to ruin my night. I want my family around me. That's all that's important. Speaking of family, have you heard from Sean yet?"

"Not since yesterday."

Emma frowned. "I texted him an hour ago, but he didn't reply," she said, worried that her younger brother wouldn't make the ceremony. Sean was a touring musician, and he'd been on the road the past six months with his band, but he'd promised to drive down from Seattle for her wedding. Unfortunately, he'd gotten caught in a snowstorm on the California-Oregon border, so he'd had to pull off the road for a few hours. "He should be here by now."

"He'll do everything he can to make it," Nicole reassured her.

"I hope so. But we both know he's not big on family events."

"Your wedding is different. Sean will be here."

"I just hope nothing has happened to him."

Nicole shook her head. "You're not normally a worrier, Emma. Where is the icy calm you display when you run into burning buildings?"

"It seems to be on vacation," she admitted. "I keep feeling an odd chill run through my body, and I don't know where it's coming from."

"Limo is here," Shayla interrupted, returning to the room with Emma's other two bridesmaids, her best friend and sister-in-law, Sara, and Drew's girlfriend, Ria. Emma had a feeling that Ria would be the next to get engaged, but Drew and Ria were pretty close-mouthed about their plans these days.

Her bridesmaids were certainly an attractive group of women, she thought. Her sisters, Nicole and Shayla, were both pretty blondes. Ria had wavy light brown hair with gold highlights, and Sara was a gorgeous brunette.

"First a toast," Sara said, handing Emma a glass of champagne. "To a fantastic friend and an incredible sister. We wish you nothing but happiness, Emma."

"To Emma," the others echoed.

"Thanks you guys," she said, blinking away another tear as she looked around the circle of females. "You all mean so much to me."

"You mean a lot to us, too," Sara said. She set down her glass and picked up Emma's bouquet of white roses. "Shall I carry these for you?"

"If you don't mind," Emma replied.

As the other bridesmaids picked up their bouquets and bags, she took one last look at herself in the mirror.

"You're gorgeous, Emma," Ria said, coming up behind her.

"Thanks." She gave Ria a sheepish smile. "I feel a little vain. I haven't looked at myself this much in years, if ever."

"You're entitled. You're the bride."

"I can only use that excuse for a few more hours."

"So where are you going on your honeymoon?" Ria asked as they headed toward the door.

"Max is surprising me. He wouldn't even let me pack my own suitcase. He had Nicole do it."

"Then you must know where they're going, Nicole," Ria said.

"Not really. I only know what clothes she's taking," Nicole replied. "Max was afraid Emma would use her interrogation skills to break me, so he only told me as much as I needed to know."

"I don't care where we go," Emma said. "And I'm not even worried about what's in my suitcase, because I'm not planning on wearing too many clothes, if you know what I mean."

Nicole laughed. "Let's go get you married."

"Finally," she said.

As she followed her sister out the door, she tried to

ignore the anxious flutter in her stomach and the goose bumps running down her arms. Everything was going to be fine. It was her wedding day. What could go wrong?

Chapter Two

"So where are you going on the honeymoon?" Spencer Harrison asked his brother, Max as they entered the bank. "You can tell me now. I won't see Emma until she meets you at the altar, so there's no way I can accidentally tell her."

Max gave him a smug smile. "I'm taking her to Paris. That's why we're here. I want to get some euros so I don't have to worry about changing money at the airport."

"Paris—nice. I'm impressed."

"Emma has never been out of the country, so we're going to do five days in Paris and five days in London. We'll be back on Christmas Eve."

"You should have stayed in Europe for Christmas."

Max shook his head. "Emma wouldn't dream of missing a Callaway family Christmas. She didn't grow up like we did, Spence. Holidays are big, joyful occasions with lots of food, family and presents. She's been shopping for cousins I've never even met. It's going to be crazy, certainly nothing like I've ever experienced."

Spencer nodded in understanding. Their parents had divorced when they were kids, and for years the holidays had been a battleground of who was supposed to go where and with which parent. His mother had usually ended up in tears at some point. Both he and Max had come to dread the season. There had been a short time in his early twenties when he'd had a different feeling about Christmas, when he'd been in love, and dreaming about a future, a family of his own, but those dreams had been crushed, too.

The last thing he was looking forward to was another holiday to remind him of how empty his life was, how much he'd lost, and how far he had to go to get any of it back. He wished he could move the calendar to January second and skip straight to the next year without having to live through holiday carols, mistletoe, and even worse, another New Year's Eve. Whoever had invented that holiday should be shot. Instead of New Year's Eve, it could have been called the night of high expectations followed by massive disappointment.

Max frowned. "You look suddenly grim. What are you thinking about?"

"Nothing." He didn't want to put his bad mood on Max, not today.

"Liar," Max said, as they got into line. "What's wrong? Is it the wedding? Are you thinking about Stephanie?"

Stephanie had been the love of his life and his fiancé, but his love for her had sent him to prison. In attempting to defend her from a stalker, he'd accidentally killed a man. In his mind, he'd acted to protect his girlfriend, but a clever and aggressive prosecutor, egged on by the wealthy family of the victim, had portrayed him as an angry, jealous boyfriend who'd been paranoid about anyone talking to Stephanie. And Stephanie hadn't been as much help as she should have been.

"Please tell me you're not still thinking about her," Max added, an irritated note in his voice. "She let you down, Spence. She's a big reason why you went to prison for seven years. I don't want to see you waste any more time thinking about her."

"I was only thinking about her because you mentioned her name. I'm not in love with her anymore. That's over."

"Seriously?" Max challenged.

"Yes. She's moved on with her life, and so have I. I have no interest in going backwards."

"I'm glad to hear that. So what's on your mind? Is it the job? You mentioned earlier that you're thinking about a change."

"I'm thinking about something," he said vaguely, not sure he was ready to talk about his plans yet.

"What?" Max asked curiously.

"I don't want to say."

"Why are you being so mysterious?"

"Because you'll probably laugh."

"Try me."

Spencer shifted his feet and dug his hands into his pockets. "Fine. You know the deli job was just supposed to be short-term, a way to make some cash while I decided what I wanted to do for a career."

"Right, so…"

"So, Gus has been letting me help in the kitchen. We don't make much at the deli beyond sandwiches, soups and the occasional pasta special, but I've discovered that I like cooking. It's creative and doesn't involve dealing with the customers, which I don't care for as much. I've been experimenting with dishes at home and toying with the idea of becoming a chef. I know it's ridiculous," he added quickly, sure he was taking the words right out of Max's mouth.

"Why do you say that? It sounds like a great idea to me, Spencer."

"I'm probably too old."

"You're thirty-seven."

"That's old for a career change."

"No, it's not. What do you need to do? Cooking school?"

"I could definitely use some training. I saw some classes I could take, and Gus has some connections in the city. He thought he could get me a job as a sous chef if I learn a few more things."

Max nodded, an approving light in his eyes. "You should do it."

"I'm thinking about it." He was already regretting sharing the plan with Max, because he could see the excitement in Max's gaze. His brother was itching to fix his life in some way, because that was Max. He liked to fix things, save people, make everything better. It's what made him a good cop. But Spencer had to find his own way to his future.

"What's to think about?" Max asked.

"It will take me years to make even a tenth of what I was making as a commodities trader."

"It's not about money. It's about doing something that makes you happy. And you just said you don't want to go backwards. So go forward. You have to start somewhere. It sucks, but it is what it is."

Max was always pragmatic, and in this instance, Spencer appreciated the lack of bullshit. "Yeah, it is what it is," he echoed. He shifted his feet and tugged at his tie.

"At least I won't have to wear suits as a chef. It's been a long time since I wore a tie. I forgot how constricting they are."

"It wasn't my idea. Emma told me the tuxes were non-negotiable."

"Emma is going to keep you on your toes."

"Agreed. She's beautiful but stubborn."

He grinned at the love in his brother's eyes. "I knew it would take someone like Emma to break down that wall around your heart. You fell hard for her."

"I tried not to, but how could I resist? She's one of a kind. You should see her in action, Spence. She charges into burning buildings like it's nothing. She's fearless and determined and a really good investigator. And you know she's taken a lot of shit being a female firefighter, but she doesn't get down when people try to put her down. She just proves them wrong."

"She's tough."

"She always tries to be, but she has a softness about her, too. Sometimes she cares too much about her cases, about the people involved." He shrugged. "But I like that about her as well. She's just the whole package."

"You're lucky you found her."

"I am lucky." He checked his watch. "I'm also late."

"You still have a few minutes. There's only one more person in front of us. How long could it take?"

Max pulled out his phone as it began to vibrate. He looked down at the screen and muttered, "Damn."

"What's wrong?"

"A case I'm working on. I need to take this. Hold my place."

"No problem."

As Max moved a few feet away to take his call, Spencer glanced at the woman standing in front of him.

Her wavy, dark red hair fell halfway down her back. She wore a black wool coat over a gray sweater, with blue jeans and black boots completing the outfit. A colorful scarf was draped around her neck. As she impatiently shifted her feet, he caught a glimpse of her profile, beautiful pale skin with a few freckles on the bridge of her nose, full pink lips, and green eyes set off by dark lashes. She was pretty. If she weren't scowling, she'd probably be even more beautiful.

His gut tightened. It was stupid as hell to feel a spark of attraction for a complete stranger. However, the fact that he could feel any spark at all was surprising. He'd been deliberately numb for a long time, because if he couldn't feel anything, then he wouldn't feel pain, and he'd had enough hurt in his life. So he'd tried to stay detached from everyone. It had been fairly easy to do. There hadn't been anyone around he wanted to attach to.

But now he was feeling hot and cold at the same time and a little off-balance. It was crazy. He didn't even know her, but he want to know her.

He'd once been good at talking to women. In high school and college he'd had more dates than he could remember, but that had been a really long time ago. He was out of practice.

But he had to start somewhere...

Giving in to impulse, he tapped her on the shoulder.

She jumped and gave him a startled look.

"What?" she demanded, anger in her eyes.

He cleared his throat, her green eyes so dazzling he couldn't think of what he wanted to say. "I was just wondering how long you've been waiting. And if this is the only line to exchange money?"

Real smooth, he thought, feeling like a complete idiot with his inane questions.

"This is it, and I've been waiting almost twenty minutes," she replied. "I didn't think there would be a line this close to the end of the day, especially on a Saturday. I can't miss my flight."

"Are you going somewhere exciting?"

She shook her head. "Excitement is the last thing I'm looking for. I just want a wide, sandy beach, a beautiful blue sea, and a lot of rum."

"Sounds like the perfect vacation," he murmured, wondering what her story was and where the shadows in her eyes had come from. "How long will you be gone?"

"As long as it takes to forget."

"Forget what?"

A shutter came down over her eyes. "Everything."

"That's a lot."

"I just want to go where no one knows me and start over. Ever have that feeling?"

"Many times," he said, meeting her gaze. "Unfortunately, it's not easy to outrun the past or ourselves. Believe me—I know."

She tilted her head, giving him a speculative look. "You don't look like a man who has anything to outrun. Unless, maybe it's your wedding…"

"I'm the best man. My brother, Max, is the groom. He's getting married in an hour and taking his bride to Paris later tonight."

"Very romantic. I hope their marriage is everything they want it to be."

"That's cryptic."

"Is it?" She shrugged. "I'm not very good at finding words these days."

"Why not?"

"That's way too long a story."

"Maybe not for this line," he said lightly.

Her frown deepened. "True. I think the man at the counter must be going around the world. He keeps asking questions about every kind of currency, some I've never even heard of." She paused as she glanced back toward the counter. "I think he's finally done. She's putting his money into an envelope."

Spencer felt an unexpected wave of disappointment that in a moment this beautiful woman would be gone, and this oddly random conversation would be over. "What's your name?" he said, feeling a need to know something more about her before she disappeared.

She hesitated. "Why do you want to know?"

"Because I do."

"Hallie Cooper. You?"

"Spencer Harrison. We should get a drink sometime."

"Do you always try to pick up women at the bank?"

He smiled at her comment. "I never pick up women at the bank—or anywhere else for that matter. It's been a while."

"Yeah? So why me?"

"You have a mirror, don't you?"

A sparkle flashed in her eyes. "You're direct."

"I sense that time is running out. What do you say— Hallie Cooper? When you come back from your trip, we could get coffee, or something with rum, in case you didn't get enough on your island. All I need is your phone number." He pulled out his phone.

"I don't know if I'm ever coming back."

"You can't lie on a beach forever."

"I'd sure like to try," she said with a sigh. "My turn," she said as the man at the counter walked away.

"Seven digits, that's all I need," he said, feeling a little desperate.

"You don't want to call me. Trust me."

"Why should I do that?"

She turned away, then flung a quick glance over her shoulder. "The last person I gave my number to ended up dead."

And with that unsettling comment, she stepped up to the counter.

He stared at her back, at the six feet of space separating them. He'd wait until she finished her money exchange, then he'd tell her he wasn't scared of ending up dead. In fact, there had been many times in the past seven years when he'd wished he were dead. Dying was sometimes easier than living. But he couldn't tell her any of that. He didn't want to scare her away.

Although, hadn't she already made it clear she wasn't interested?

Actually, he thought she was interested. She was just scared.

Scared of what he wondered? What had happened to make her want to run to the other end of the world and never come back?

"Looks like we're next," Max said, returning to his side.

"Yeah," he said distractedly, his gaze still on Hallie.

"What is it with you and redheads, Spence?"

He smiled. "I like the fire. She's beautiful, don't you think?"

"Did you get her number?"

"Not yet, but I haven't given up."

"Good for you. It's about time you got back in the game."

He didn't know about getting back in the game, but he did know that he felt a compelling need to not let this woman walk out of his life without another word.

As he waited for Hallie to finish her business, he

glanced around the bank, noting the holiday garlands, poinsettias and the Christmas tree in the corner. Christmas was less than two weeks away, and there was a festive atmosphere in the air, which probably had as much to do with closing being minutes away as with the upcoming holidays. There was only one other customer at the main bank of teller windows, and two female loan officers were chatting by one of their desks.

He was about to look away when the front door opened, and two men walked in. They were probably in their twenties or thirties. Both wore jeans. One had a gray sweatshirt with a hoodie pulled over his head and sunglasses covering his eyes. The other had on a black jacket and a Yankee baseball cap, his eyes also hidden by dark lenses. These two did not want to be recognized. Why? He suddenly had a bad feeling.

One man lingered by the door as the other got in line, waiting for the last customer to finish at the main counter. As the older woman left the teller window and headed out of the bank, the guy in line seemed to exchange some sort of signal with the man by the door. Then he stepped up to the waiting bank teller, a young Asian woman.

Spencer frowned, looking around for a security guard, but there was no one in sight. "Shit!" he muttered.

Max gave him a surprised look. "What's wrong?"

"We've got trouble."

Spencer had barely finished speaking when the man by the door turned the dead bolt and pulled out a gun. "Don't move. Don't anybody move," he yelled.

Chapter Three

As the limo passed by the front of the church, Emma could see her grandparents and parents standing on the steps, welcoming their guests. She hadn't wanted a huge wedding, but being part of the Callaway family had made anything small impossible. She was not only one of eight siblings; she had over twenty cousins, and a dozen aunts and uncles. Along with family, came the fire department, which was her second family, and quite a few members of the police department, who were Max's second family. So they'd given up on trying to cut down the guest list and decided to have a big crowd and a night to remember.

"Is Max ready to deal with all the Callaways?" Nicole asked.

"He's getting used to the constant crowd," she replied. "His mother is a little overwhelmed though. She seemed very nervous at the rehearsal dinner last night."

"She's been nervous every time I've seen her," Nicole commented.

Emma nodded. "Susan is high strung and emotional. She drives Max crazy with her drama. He's been taking care of her ever since his dad took off. And I guess she was even worse while Spencer was in prison. She's a sweet woman though. She just gets overwhelmed with what are usually little problems."

"What's the deal with Max's father? Is he coming today?"

"Max didn't invite him. He said his dad hasn't been part of his life, so why should he be part of his wedding? I can understand that feeling. I should have stuck with not inviting our father," she added, unable to keep the bitter note out of her voice. She'd spent weeks debating whether or not to invite her biological father to the wedding. He'd deserted her and Nicole and their mother, Lynda, when Emma was a toddler, and while there had been some sporadic contact over the years, she didn't think of him as a father. Jack Callaway was her dad. He was the one who'd been there through all the important moments of her life.

"I'm sorry," Nicole said quietly, meeting her gaze. "I know you invited him at my urging. I thought it would be a good opportunity for you to reconnect."

"He wasn't interested in reconnecting. He's never been interested in me at all."

"That's not true."

"It is, Nicole. You share his love of history and teaching, but he doesn't understand me, and I don't understand him. It's fine. I just wish I hadn't given him another chance to reject me. I shouldn't have wasted all that time worrying about whether or not to invite him. He was never going to come."

"Don't let his absence spoil the day."

"It won't. I'm actually glad he's not here. Jack is the only father I need." She paused. "It's weird that Max and I both have a history of deadbeat dads, isn't it? Although, you and I got lucky when Mom married Jack. He's always treated us like his daughters."

"I wonder why Max's mom didn't remarry."

"I don't think she ever got over Max's dad leaving her."

The limo came to a stop.

"Showtime," Shayla said. "Are you ready, Emma?"

"More than ready," she replied. The chauffeur helped her out of the car, and she moved quickly into the hallway where her wedding planner and cousin, Cynthia Callaway, waiting for them. Cynthia was a tall, willowy brunette who moved and talked at a very fast pace. She was extremely efficient and very organized. She'd taken care of every detail of the wedding and reception, and Emma didn't know what she would have done without her.

Cynthia waved them into a small room. "You can wait here until we're ready."

"Is everyone here?" Emma asked.

"The pews are filling up," Cynthia answered. "But we still have fifteen minutes."

"Any sign of Sean?"

Cynthia shook her head. "Not yet. I texted him a few minutes ago, but I got no reply. Thank goodness he's not one of the ushers. We won't have to hold up the wedding for him."

"I know he's not in the bridal party, but I still want him to see me get married."

"Then he better get here in the next fifteen minutes," Cynthia said. "There's another ceremony after yours, Emma, so we can't wait forever, but I promise we'll wait as long as we can. I'll go check again."

"Thanks." Emma had barely entered the dressing room when her bridesmaids began to disappear: Nicole to check on the ring-bearers—her son Brandon and Brandon's brother, Kyle, Sara to make sure her one-month-old baby girl didn't need a feeding, and Ria, who wanted to make sure that her niece, Megan was all set to be the flower girl and accompany the ring bearers down the aisle, which left Shayla.

"I think you should touch up your lips," Shayla said.

"Why? Max is only going to kiss it off."

Shayla laughed. "Not until the end of the ceremony. Think of all the photos before that moment."

"Fine. I'll add some more lipstick. But that's it. I want Max to recognize me after all."

"Shoot, I left my makeup bag in the limo. I'll get it."

As Shayla left, Emma's grandmother, Eleanor Callaway walked into the room. Eleanor was an attractive older woman with platinum blonde hair and blue eyes that were sometimes sharp and sometimes lost, as she battled Alzheimer's.

"Grandma," Emma said, giving her a hug. "I'm so glad you're here."

"Me, too." Eleanor waved her hand toward her husband, Patrick, who was hovering in the doorway. "Leave us be. I want to talk to Emma for a few minutes."

"I'll be right outside," Patrick replied. "Don't be long."

"I won't be." Eleanor took Emma's hands and gave her a smile. "You look gorgeous."

"Thank you. So do you." Emma was happy to see a sharp gleam in her grandmother's eyes. "How are you feeling today?"

"Like my old self."

"I'm glad."

"I don't know how long it will last, so I want to give you this before I forget what it is or who you are," she said with a touch of painful humor. Eleanor opened her gold clutch purse and pulled out a dark blue velvet box. "My grandmother gave me this when I married your grandfather, and I thought you might want to wear it—it could be your *something old*."

Emma took the jewelry box out of her grandmother's hand and opened the lid. A beautiful gold heart with a sapphire diamond in the middle hung on a thin gold chain and sparkled in its velvet setting. "Oh, Grandma," she breathed, as she took out the necklace. "It's gorgeous."

"My grandmother told me it would bring me luck in my marriage as it brought her luck. She was married for forty-three years before she passed away. And your grandpa and I are going on sixty-two years together."

"I have a feeling it took more than a little luck for you to stay together that long," Emma murmured.

"Oh, it took work, for sure," Eleanor said with a nod. "Your grandpa isn't the easiest man to live with."

"You don't have to tell me that." She adored her grandfather, but she was not unaware of the fact that he could be angry and arrogant on occasion.

She handed her grandmother the jewelry box and put the necklace on. It was perfect for her sweetheart neckline. She had debated on what to wear around her neck for a long time, but she hadn't had the right necklace until now. "How does it look?"

Eleanor gave an approving smile. "Like it was made for you." She glanced around the empty room. "Where is everyone?"

Emma shrugged. "Who knows? But I'm happy to have a moment alone with you. Thank you so much for this, Grandma."

"You're welcome. I gave Nicole a ring from my mother when she got married, and I have something special for Shayla when it's her day." She paused. "I have to say Emma that you remind me the most of myself. I know we're not related by blood, but I feel so close to you. I always have, from the first minute your father brought Lynda to the house and introduced me to you."

"I don't remember that."

"You were just a toddler, but you were so curious and stubborn that I knew Jack would have his hands full with you. Now it's Max's turn."

She smiled. "Yes, it is. But Max has a stubborn streak, too. So I may have my hands full with him."

"He's a good man, a strong man, someone you can count on, lean on; I like him very much."

"So do I."

"Do you want to know the secret to love and a long marriage, Emma?"

"Boy, do I," she said with a laugh.

"Don't keep score. Being right won't keep you warm at night."

"That's good advice."

"And be kind to each other," Eleanor added, her expression growing more serious. "We're all flawed, Emma. Even the best of men can sometimes make a terrible mistake."

Emma's gut tightened. "Is there something you want to tell me, Grandma?" Eleanor had been alluding to some secret in her past for the last several months, but she never stayed sharp enough to get the whole story out.

"No, dear," Eleanor said quickly.

"Are you sure? I feel like you've wanted to tell us something about Grandpa, maybe about something bad that happened in the past. You keep talking about a secret that you don't want to keep anymore."

Eleanor stared back at her, a glint in her eyes. "What else have I said about this secret?"

"Nothing specific, but whatever it is, it seems to bother you. You get agitated and upset."

"I wish I knew what you're talking about, Emma, but this condition I have—it's like I have blackouts. I'm there, and then I'm gone for a while. When I come back, sometimes it's been five minutes, and sometimes it's been five weeks."

"I'm sorry," Emma said quickly, seeing the frustration in Eleanor's eyes now. "I shouldn't have mentioned it."

"It's all right. I just hope whatever I say doesn't hurt the people I love, especially your grandfather. He's always stood by me."

"And you've stood by him."

"That's what a wife does, Emma."

"Even if a husband does something wrong?" she asked, knowing she should drop it, but how many times would she have a chance to speak this honestly with her grandmother?

"Emma, you should let it go."

"I know I should, but remember what you said about me being curious and stubborn?"

Eleanor sighed. "Everything your grandfather has done in his life has been done out of love for his family and his friends. This isn't the time to talk about the past, Emma. Tonight you begin a new life, a life with Max, and you don't need to be thinking about anything else."

"I just want to help you. I feel like you want to tell the family something, and every time you start to do that, Grandpa shuts you up. If something is troubling you, you can tell me."

"Thank you, Emma. But nothing is bothering me, at least nothing I can remember at the moment," she added with a small smile.

Before Eleanor could say more, Cynthia and Nicole

returned to the dressing room. They both looked a little too serious, and Emma's pulse quickened. "What's wrong?" she asked.

"I'm sure he's just running late," Cynthia said.

Emma saw Cynthia and Nicole exchange a quick look. "Sean still isn't here yet?"

"It's not Sean we're worried about. Well, not *just* Sean," Cynthia amended. "Max isn't here yet, either. Or his brother."

Her heart skipped a beat. "What do you mean Max isn't here yet? I talked to him a little over an hour ago. He said that he and Spencer were going to leave in a few minutes."

"There's no sign of either of them," Nicole replied.

"Did anyone call Max?" she asked.

Cynthia shook her head.

"Well, give me a phone."

Cynthia handed over her phone, and Emma punched in Max's number. The phone rang six times before voice mail came on. The bad feeling she'd been fighting all day came back with a vengeance. "He's not answering."

"He's probably in the car, driving over here," Nicole put in, forced optimism in her voice. "He'll be here any second."

"Right," she said, trying to rein in her fearful thoughts. Max wouldn't be late to his wedding. Where was he? And why wasn't he answering his phone?

Chapter Four

Hallie Cooper's heart pounded against her chest as she dropped to her knees in front of the counter, hands in the air, as instructed by the two men in the process of robbing the bank. Her pulse was going way too fast, and terror had tightened her chest. She struggled to breathe, to stay on her knees, to think through the fear, to focus on the current minute and not the one about to come. But even as her therapist's words rang through her head, her brain screamed in shock that this wasn't supposed to be happening. She wasn't supposed to be facing another gun or more evil. She was supposed to be safe now, the bad stuff behind her.

She just hoped it would all be over fast, a quick grab of cash and then they'd be gone. The man with the Yankee baseball cap stood at the counter, instructing the teller to fill a canvas bag with cash from the drawers. The second guy in the hooded sweatshirt was making his way around the bank, collecting cell phones, jewelry, and wallets from the customers and employees. He was in front of Spencer now. She watched as Spencer pulled off his watch and tossed his wallet into the bag.

As his brother pulled out his phone, it began to ring. The man hesitated.

"In the bag," the gunman ordered. "And your wallet, too."

Spencer's brother reluctantly handed over his phone and wallet, his expression grim.

And then it was her turn.

As the man moved towards her, she could see his hand on the gun. One slight pull of the trigger, and it would be all over. She knew what a bullet could do, how it could rip apart a body, destroy a life. She'd dealt with more gunshot wounds than she could count. She'd spent the past four years as a nurse in the Army and done two tours in Afghanistan. She'd seen more horror in those years than anyone should see in a lifetime, and she was still haunted by terrifying images. The most innocent sound could set her off, a rumble of thunder, a car backfire, the snap of a branch. Post-traumatic stress syndrome was the official diagnosis, but giving her panic a name hadn't done much to stop the attacks.

She lifted her gaze from the gun to the man's face. She couldn't see his eyes, but she could see the tension in his jaw, the barely restrained energy in his stance, and the nasty looking snake tattoo on his neck. He was on edge, maybe on some kind of drug. She didn't think it would take much to make him snap.

"What are you looking at?" he grumbled.

"Nothing," she muttered, immediately realizing her mistake. She handed over her bag and looked back down at the ground, telling herself not to be stupid. If this guy thought she could recognize him or pick him out of a line-up, she would be in more danger.

Her heart beat even faster as she felt his gaze on her head, and then finally he stepped away and ordered the teller who'd been helping her to come around the counter and get on the ground next to her.

The older woman scurried around the wall and dropped to her knees a few feet away from Hallie. She looked absolutely terrified.

The hooded gunman glanced back at his partner. "Almost done?"

"Getting there. Check the door."

As the man closest to Hallie moved away, she saw Spencer give her a reassuring look. A few minutes ago she'd been thinking that it had been a long time since a handsome stranger had hit on her. And when he'd asked for her number, for one brief second she'd been tempted. If it hadn't been her turn at the counter, maybe she would have given it to him. But more likely she would have said no and walked away, because she wasn't ready to invest in anyone or anything, not even in a casual way. She needed to get over the massive hurt in her heart first. How long that would take, she didn't know.

She'd planned to start her recovery tomorrow, on a beach in the middle of nowhere, and hopefully find some much-needed peace. Her tropical island was calling to her now. Her flight was leaving in less than two hours. She was so close to escape and yet so far away.

She'd never imagined that coming to the bank to exchange her money would put her life in danger. While she'd been prepared to die every day that she'd served in the Army, she was not prepared to die now. It would be the worst kind of irony to have escaped the bombs and gunfire that had killed her fiancé only to lose her life in a bank in the middle of an upscale neighborhood in San

Francisco.

It wasn't going to happen, she told herself. These guys just wanted money and then they'd be gone. A few more minutes, and this would all be over.

A phone began to ring again, the sound coming from the canvas bag where they had tossed their cell phones. Spencer's brother stiffened. She could see the frustration on his face, and she felt for him.

Was the bride waiting at the church, wondering where her groom was?

Hopefully not. Hopefully, the wedding wasn't for a few more hours, but Hallie could see the longing in the groom's eyes. He wanted to answer that phone. She hoped he wouldn't try to get to it. She didn't want anyone to do anything to anger the gunmen. If they followed instructions, no one would get hurt.

* * *

"Don't be a hero," Spencer muttered to Max, seeing the tension in his brother's eyes. "Better we get there late than not at all."

"That's Emma calling. I know it is. She's wondering where the hell I am. I wish I had my gun."

"Well, you don't, so don't do anything stupid."

"I'm usually the one telling you that."

That was true. Max had always had more control than Spencer, but today his brother had a lot on the line.

Looking away from Max, he turned his gaze to the hooded man, who was now digging through the bag to turn off the offending cell phone. He was pissed off and agitated by the persistent ringing. Every movement he made was jerky, nervous. It was clear he was high on something. Spencer wasn't surprised. Drugs and desperation fueled a lot of robberies. He'd spent seven years of his life locked up with guys like this—exactly like this, he realized, as the man lifted his arm to wipe some sweat off his forehead. The gesture revealed a tattoo on his wrist.

The tattoo consisted of five dots, which comprised the five points of a star. It was a common prison tattoo, the outer dots representing the walls of the jail, the inside dot the prisoner. He had a similar tattoo on his wrist. It had hurt like a son of a bitch, but getting it done had made his life a little easier on the inside. He'd become one of them. It was not a group he had ever imagined joining.

He'd grown up in the suburbs, graduated from UC Berkeley, worked on Wall Street. He'd had money and clothes and a damn good life until the bottom had fallen out of it. But he'd had to bury that side of himself when he went to prison. He'd had to change in order to survive the culture. Now he was going to have to change again, find out who he was, somewhere between where he used to be and where he was now. But first he had to get out of this bank.

He glanced at Max again. He could see the wheels turning in his brother's head. Max was assessing the situation, weighing the pros and cons of two armed gunmen versus four bank employees and three customers. He was thinking like a cop, debating whether or not he could personally take down both guys without losing anyone in the process.

Spencer didn't think that was possible. The best scenario was to stay quiet and hope the robbers took off as quickly as they'd come. But not doing anything went against Max's nature.

Max had wanted to be a cop for as long as Spencer could remember. His younger brother had always had some innate need for justice. A shrink would probably say his brother's need to put away the bad guys was somehow related to their father's abandonment, but that seemed too simplistic for Spencer's taste. The truth was more than that.

Maybe Max did feel good when he took a criminal off the street, but he also liked the chase, the puzzle, and the adrenaline rush. And he was good at what he did.

Spencer respected Max's achievements. It had taken him awhile to get past the anger he'd felt toward Max for not being able to save him from prison, but in retrospect he knew that Max had done all he could. And his anger with his brother had just been a part of his overwhelming sense of injustice. But that anger was gone now. He was happy to have his brother back in his life, and he'd been honored when Max had asked him to be his best man. He wanted nothing more than to stand beside Max when he and Emma exchanged vows.

His thoughts turned to the wedding. Emma had to be worried about Max, and his mom was probably already crying hysterical tears. Susan Harrison had always been a drama queen. He couldn't imagine what they thought was going on. But they'd explain everything when they got to the church and one day this would just be a crazy story to tell.

"Damn," Max said, his jaw tightening

He followed Max's gaze to the female loan officer who was surreptitiously moving closer to her desk. There was a focus in her gaze. She was trying to get to something—an alarm maybe. He wanted to yell at her to stop, that losing the bank's money wasn't worth losing her life. In five minutes, these guys would be gone. They just had to wait it out.

He wanted to find a way to get her attention, but she

was zoned in completely on her goal, so deep in concentration that she didn't see the hooded gunman turn and look right at her.

"Stop," the gunman yelled, raising his gun.

The woman froze for a second. Then she reached for her computer keyboard and pushed a key.

Shit!

Spencer started to his feet, but he was a split second behind Max, who tackled the woman to the ground just as the gun went off.

Screams lit up the air as Max fell to the ground, clutching his side, blood staining the front of his white shirt.

Spencer rushed toward his brother, and a bullet whizzed past his ear. He knelt down beside Max. His brother looked up at him with anguish in his eyes. "Emma," he murmured. "Tell Emma I love her. Tell her I'm sorry I screwed things up."

"No, you're going to tell her yourself." He glanced at the gunman, seeing the wild light in the man's eyes. The adrenaline rush had lit him up like the Christmas tree in the corner of the bank. It was surprising he hadn't shot all of them. "He needs help."

"I don't give a shit what he needs," the man replied. "And I didn't tell you that you could move."

"He's my brother."

"What did you do?" the second gunman interrupted, anger on his face. "Why did you shoot him?"

"He got in the way. She was going for the alarm. I had to stop her." He aimed his gun at the woman now cowering and crying by the side of her desk. "Bitch."

"I'm sorry," she whispered, tears streaming down her face, as she put her hands in a silent plea for mercy.

"Leave her alone. Let's get out of here," the other

gunman said. He'd barely finished speaking when sirens lit up the air.

Spencer could see the panic flash across their faces. Their escape route had just been cut off. The hooded man walked over to the windows. "Cops everywhere." He started pulling the blinds closed. The man in the Yankee cap moved over to the door to see what was happening out front.

While the men were preoccupied with the cops, Spencer took off his coat and covered Max's legs. His brother was going into shock and blood was gushing from his wound. He put his hands over the injury, applying as much pressure as he could.

His brother groaned from the painful pressure.

"Sorry, but I need to slow this bleeding down," Spencer said.

"It's not going to work. You have to take care of Emma. Tell her how happy she made me. Promise me."

"Don't die on me," Spencer said forcefully, fear running through his body as Max's eyes closed. "Hang in there, Max. Emma needs you. I need you, too."

His words went unheard. Max was unconscious.

A loud speaker suddenly crackled. The voice of a police officer ordered the men to come out with their hands up.

"What are we going to do?" the hooded man asked, meeting his partner in the middle of the bank.

"Bargain," the man said. "We've got hostages to trade for an escape."

"They're not going to deal."

"They'll have to if they don't want everyone in here to die."

The phone on one of the desks began to ring. The men didn't budge.

"If you want to negotiate, you should answer that," Spencer said.

"Did I say you could talk?" the hooded man demanded.

He ignored that comment, determined to find a way to get Max some help. "Yu have to offer them something, a sign of good faith. Let me get my brother out of here. You don't want him to die."

"I don't give a shit if he dies."

"Yes, you do. Bank robbery beats a murder rap. I know what I'm talking about." He pulled back his sleeve and lifted his arm, showing his tattoo. "You can still get out of here. You can negotiate an escape car, but if this guy dies, you're done. Let me carry him out of here."

The guy in the Yankee cap looked like he was considering the suggestion, but the hooded man shook his head. "No way. We need everyone for insurance." He looked back at his partner. "You agree, right?"

The other man slowly nodded, and Spencer's heart sank.

"Everyone against the wall, over there," the man in the Yankee cap said.

The employees and customers quickly moved toward the nearby wall, but Spencer wasn't about to take his hands off of Max.

"You, too," the hooded man said, waving his weapon at Spencer.

"I'm not leaving my brother. At least let me try to keep him alive."

"He's not important," Yankee cap said. "Let him be."

The hooded man frowned but followed his partner's lead. They moved further away to discuss their options.

Spencer pressed his hands down harder on Max's

wound. "Hang in there, Max," he whispered. "Emma needs you. And so do I."

Chapter Five

The man on the floor was going to die, Hallie thought, seeing the blood pooling under Max's body. He was going to bleed out right here on the floor of the bank. Her head spun with the realization, with the horror to come. Spencer was going to lose his brother. The groom was never going to get to his bride. It was tragic. And it had all happened so incredibly fast.

She wanted to help. The nurse inside of her *needed* to help, but what could she do? She'd been ordered to stay put. And even if she hadn't, she'd given up on medicine months ago. She'd told herself that never again would she be faced with a life and death situation—never again would someone's entire existence be in her hands, because she wasn't up to the task. She'd let down her profession, her father, and herself. And she just wanted to put it all behind her.

But there was a man in front of her who was dying. And Spencer didn't know exactly what to do. He was trying, but he wasn't getting it done.

She licked her lips, fighting the panic still running around in her head. She could do this. She could try to help, she told herself.

And then the hooded gunman suddenly pulled out his gun and started shooting.

She instinctively hit the ground, heart pounding, waiting for the explosion of pain. But all she heard was a shower of glass. She slowly lifted her gaze, realizing that the man had simply shot out the security cameras.

She tried to breathe, but it seemed almost impossible to take in air. The people next to her were crying. One of the women was praying. She felt like doing both, but in the past neither crying nor praying had gotten her anywhere.

Max was whispering to his brother, encouraging him to fight. Maybe she needed to fight, too. She cleared her throat, but her voice still came out scratchy and rough. "You need to make a compress," she said to Spencer.

Spencer looked at her, and she could see the fear in his eyes, but also the determination, and it gave her courage. "Can I help him?" she said more loudly, drawing the Yankee-capped gunman's gaze to her. "I'm a nurse."

He gave her a long look, then shrugged. "Fine."

Hallie got up and moved quickly to Spencer's side. She pulled the scarf off of her neck and bundled it up. Spencer lifted his fingers, and she shoved the material under his hands. "More pressure," she said. "Use the heels of your hands." As Spencer did as instructed, she took off her coat and threw it over Max's upper torso, wanting to keep him as warm as possible.

The phone on the desk rang again. The two men still didn't answer it.

She looked at Spencer. "They don't know what to do," she whispered, realizing that the robbers' indecision and inexperience might make this situation even worse.

"No," he agreed. "We have to find a way to make them work with the cops. My brother can't die, Hallie. He's getting married today."

"Then we need to do something fast," she said, meeting his gaze.

"It's bad, isn't it?"

She couldn't count how many times someone had asked her that question, how many times she'd had to crush a dream. She'd told herself she was done with all that, but here she was again. And her only answer was the truth. "Yes, it's bad."

* * *

Emma stood by the small window in the dressing room at the church. She had her arms wrapped around her waist, but she was still cold—icy cold. Fear and worry knotted her stomach, bringing nausea along with the chill. Something was terribly wrong. It was now thirty minutes past when the ceremony was supposed to start, but there was no sign of Max. He wasn't answering his phone. In fact, it appeared that he had turned it off, because now it went straight to voice mail. If he had turned it off, then he'd seen her number on the screen, and he'd chosen not to talk to her. But that didn't make sense.

Max wanted to marry her. He'd told her just last night that he'd never been this happy in his entire life. And he'd kissed her like he was never going to let her go. But he had let her go, because they'd decided to spend the night before their wedding apart. She'd gone home to her parents' house while he'd stayed in the apartment they shared. Now, she wished those hours back. Had something happened during the night? Had he been suddenly filled with doubts? Had he changed his mind about wanting to get married?

No, she told herself firmly. She'd spoken to him a few hours ago, and he'd joked that she probably wouldn't recognize him in his tux, because he was more a jeans and jacket kind of guy. There hadn't been a hint of anything wrong in his voice.

She drew in a shaky breath and let it out as she watched the parking lot. It was full. No vehicles were moving. Everything had come to a standstill. The guests were still packed in the church—waiting...

And she was alone. She'd ordered everyone out of the dressing room, because she couldn't stand the pitying looks or the endless reassurances. She loved her family, but at this moment the only person she needed was Max.

The door behind her opened. It wasn't Max who entered the room, but Nicole. At her silent question, Nicole shook her head. "He's still not here, Emma. But there are a lot of people looking for him."

"He didn't stand me up, Nic."

"I don't think he did."

"Which means something happened to him."

Nicole gave a helpless, frustrated shake of her head. "I don't know." She paused, hesitation in her eyes.

"What?" Emma demanded, knowing there was something else on Nicole's mind.

"There's another ceremony scheduled for seven-thirty tonight."

"What does that mean?"

"The priest said we can hold the church until seven. That's another forty minutes. I'm sure Max will arrive by then."

She wanted Nicole's words to make her feel better, but they didn't. The reminder of time passing only made the fear worse. "I'm scared," she whispered. "Max is never late. I'm the one who runs behind schedule. He's always waiting for me."

"Try to stay positive. I know that's not going to be easy."

"It's impossible."

"Max loves you, Emma. He's going to find a way to get to you, no matter what has happened."

The door opened again, and Emma could see her family hovering in the hallway, but it was her father, Jack Callaway, and Max's mother, Susan Harrison, who made their way into the room. Susan was crying. At the look on her future mother-in-law's face, Emma felt another wave of terror, and she reached for Nicole's hand for support. "What's happened?" she asked.

"Max's car was located in the lot behind the bank three blocks from here," Jack said.

"He's at the bank?" she asked. "Isn't it closed by now?"

"Yes." Jack stepped forward and put his hands on her shoulders. "The bank was robbed just before closing, Emma, and it's turned into a hostage situation. Max and Spencer are inside."

"Oh, my God!" She put a hand to her heart. "But he's all right, isn't he?"

"I assume so. They haven't let any of the hostages go yet. The negotiations are just beginning."

"Let's go to the bank," she said immediately.

"Emma—"

She shook her head at her father, not letting him finish. "I am not going to stay here and wait. I want to be there when Max comes out. I need to be there. Please don't argue with me."

"I'll take you there," he said.

"Thank you."

Her mom took off her coat and handed it to her. "At least wear this, Emma. It's cold outside."

Emma pulled the coat on over her wedding dress and followed her father to the door, telling herself with every step that Max was going to be fine. He was a cop. He knew how to handle himself. At the same time, she worried that because he was a cop, he could be in more danger. At least Spencer was with him. They might have had their differences in the past, but she knew Spencer would do everything he could to protect his brother.

* * *

"They're on something," Hallie murmured, watching the gunmen pace around the bank, their movements nervous and agitated.

"Which makes them more dangerous," Spencer said, his expression grim. "They're not thinking rationally."

"Why aren't they talking to the cops?" The phone had rung three times in the past five minutes. A hostage negotiator had gotten on a loudspeaker telling them that the bank was surrounded and to pick up the phone. But so far the gunmen had done nothing more than argue with each other.

"They don't know what to ask for."

"Does it matter what they ask for? The cops aren't going to give it to them, are they?"

"Maybe they will, if they want to keep the rest of us alive."

She swallowed hard at the thought of more gunshots, more blood, more death. She was barely keeping it together, but she couldn't lose it now. Later—later, she'd break down, let go. Hopefully by then she'd be on her beautiful island in the middle of the ocean, letting the sun soak away her troubles, and the rum flow through her veins bringing peace and forgetfulness.

But her island image was hard to cling to when she looked down at the man on the floor. Max's face was ashen, and while the blood flow had slowed down, it was still seeping through the scarf and Spencer's fingers.

"Press down a little harder," she said.

Spencer frowned. "I'm hurting him."

"No, you're saving him, trust me."

"You've worked on gunshot wounds?"

"More than I can count. I was an Army nurse."

"Was?"

"I got tired of watching people die." The stark words came out of her mouth before she could stop them.

Spencer stared back at her. "My brother can't die, Hallie. Max is the good one. I'm the screw-up. It should be me on the floor, but Max had to be the hero. He had to try to save that woman."

"I think he did save her, if that's any consolation."

"I should have jumped up first. I saw her going for the alarm. I just didn't want to draw attention to her. But if I'd moved—"

"You can't change what happened. I've been down the endless road of 'what ifs'. It doesn't get you anywhere."

"You're probably right." He looked away from her to the gunmen. The men weren't paying them any attention, too wrapped up in their own discussion of what to do next. Turning back to her, he said, "What happened, Hallie?"

She didn't know how to answer that question. "A million things."

"Give me one."

"Well, the worst thing was watching my boyfriend die and knowing that he wouldn't have been where he was if I hadn't wanted to talk to him. He would have been far away from the bomb blast if it weren't for me. And I've gone over that night so many times in my mind, thinking how one different decision would have changed it all. But like I said, playing that game doesn't make anything better."

"I'm sorry."

She shrugged, because nothing he could say would take the pain away. It was her constant companion.

"Wrong place, wrong time, doesn't make you to blame, Hallie."

"Maybe. But that wasn't the only thing I did wrong that night." She paused. "I'm not the good one, either."

He met her gaze. "Hard to believe."

That's because he didn't know her, didn't know the depth to which she'd sunk. Her own father could barely look at her now. All her life she'd tried to live up to his very high bar, but she'd fallen short. It was another reason why she wanted to escape. The last place she wanted to be at the holidays was with her family.

She shook her father's disapproving image out of her mind and focused on Max. She wished she could do more for him, but he needed surgery. They just had to keep him alive until they could get him to the hospital.

"The bleeding is slowing down," Spencer said.

She didn't know if that were true or just Spencer's wishful thinking. But she did know if this didn't end soon, Max wasn't going to make it to his wedding or to his bride.

Chapter Six

Emma spent her days racing to fire scenes. She was no stranger to sirens, crime scene tape, or strobe lights, but the beams bouncing off the dark buildings in the commercial area surrounding the bank got her heart pounding even faster. She was not going to a job; she was going to Max, and that changed everything.

The police had closed off the street, so her father double parked about a block away, and they jumped out of the car. As her feet hit the pavement, she was assailed by a wave of terror that almost knocked her down. But she forced herself to keep moving. She had to find out what was happening.

As they neared the command post, she saw the SWAT van, and the enormous police presence outside the bank, and the knot in her throat grew bigger. She wasn't surprised at the show of force. Max was a cop. The department would work as hard as they could to bring him out safely.

A tall, dark-haired man wearing body armor approached them as they ducked under the police tape. She recognized him immediately. It was Brady O'Neal, who played basketball with both Max and her brother, Burke. Brady was a hostage negotiator, and she didn't like the somber expression in his eyes. "Brady, what's happening? Is Max in there?"

"We believe so," Brady said, his mouth drawn in a tight line. "His car is in the lot. We haven't been able to make contact with the gunmen yet."

"How many are inside?" her father cut in.

"We're not sure. The security cameras went out when we arrived, but the techs are working on getting the video up until that point. We should have it soon."

"How do you know they have guns?" she asked.

His lips tightened. "Several passerby reported shots fired."

Her stomach turned over. "God," she breathed.

"Don't go to the worst scenario," he said quickly. "We don't know anything yet."

"Max wouldn't stand by and do nothing if someone was shooting."

"He also wouldn't do something stupid," Brady said. "He's an experienced cop." He gave her a long, commiserating look. "I'm sorry, Emma."

"We were supposed to be married by now, having our first dance, making our first toast," she said. "I had this feeling earlier that it was all too good to be true. I was right."

"You weren't right," her father said. "You're going to marry Max, and you're going to be happy." He let his words sink in, then added. "I'm going to talk to Henry, see what he knows." Henry was another cop and one of her father's closest friends. While the cops and firefighters had a friendly rivalry in the city, when it came to taking care of each other, they were all brothers.

A man stuck his head out of the SWAT van. "Brady, we've got a feed."

"Stay here," Brady said, then ran toward the back of the van.

She hesitated for one second, then followed him up the steps. The cops inside were too busy looking at the monitor to notice her presence.

On the video, two men with guns could be seen walking back and forth in the middle of the bank. A teller was collecting cash. And in the corner of the shot, she could see Max and Spencer on their knees, hands in the air. She felt a wave of relief. They were okay.

Then everything changed. Someone moved, a flash of red in the corner of the screen. Max jumped to his feet. A gun went off. He stumbled and fell to the ground, blood spattering across his dress shirt as Spencer rushed to his side.

"Oh, my God," she whispered in horror.

Brady turned around and hustled her out of the van.

"That was Max. He's hurt," she said. "They shot him, Brady."

"I know," he said, giving her a little shake. "You need to stay here, let us do our job, Emma."

"I want to help."

"Then don't get in the way."

"You have to save him, Brady. You have to. Promise me."

"I'm going to do everything I can," he said grimly.

It wasn't a promise, but it was all she was going to get.

* * *

Spencer stared down at Max's face. It appeared that his brother's skin was taking on the faint hue of blue, or was that just the strobe lights flashing through the upper portion of the uncovered windows? He looked over at Hallie, needing her reassurance.

Her face was tense, her jaw tight, her eyes filled with determination but also fear. She was checking Max's pulse and after a moment she nodded. "He's hanging in there."

A part of him wondered if she was telling him a comforting lie, but he chose instead to believe her words, because any other scenario was too terrifying to contemplate. He shifted his body as his legs began to cramp from the tight position. He was careful to keep the pressure on Max's wound. Thankfully, the bleeding had slowed down.

He glanced across the bank where the men were in yet another discussion about whether or not they should answer the phone. He was desperate for them to get the negotiations started, to take some sort of action. It was Max's only chance. But these idiots didn't know what to do. "We had to get the stupidest bank robbers on the planet," he muttered angrily.

"I wouldn't tell them that," Hallie replied.

"Maybe I should. They need some advice."

"They're not going to take it from you. Unless…" She paused. "You showed them a tattoo before. What does it mean?"

"It's a prison tattoo, the same one the hooded guy has on his arm."

"You were in prison?" she asked, surprise in her eyes.

"For seven years. Manslaughter. I killed the man who was stalking my fiancé," he added, making short work of a long story.

"Sounds justified. How did you end up in jail?"

He could hear the doubt in her voice, and he wasn't surprised. Everyone had questioned his side of the story. "It's a long story."

"Tell me at least part of it."

"I can't. I have to think of a way out of this."

"There's no way out, Spencer, not unless they pick up the phone and start talking to the cops."

"How can I make them do that?"

"You already tried. Let's just do what we're doing." She drew in a shaky breath. "I feel sick."

"Hang in there," he said, seeing the distress in her eyes.

"I'm trying. I could really use a distraction from all the blood."

He hesitated, taking another quick look across the bank. Their captors weren't paying them any attention. They were confident they had this group under control, and they did. Spencer was the only one who could probably do something, and he couldn't take his hands off of Max's abdomen.

"Spencer," Hallie said. "Please talk to me."

"Okay. I'll tell you what happened to me. There was a guy who was harassing my fiancé, one of her coworkers. He would follow her, take pictures of her walking down the street and send them to her. One night I saw him outside of our apartment. Stephanie wasn't home. He was waiting in the shadows for her, but he got me instead. I confronted him. He gave me a smug smile and said something to the effect of having my fiancé. I hit him. One punch, and he went down. He hit his head on the sidewalk and died in the hospital an hour later."

Hallie stared back at him with wide eyes, but so far there was no hint of disgust, so he went on. "The prosecutor twisted what happened between us, and he persuaded the jury that I was paranoid, jealous and angry enough to kill an innocent man who was interested in my girlfriend. The man wasn't innocent, but he was clever, smarter than me. He'd covered his tracks."

"But your fiancé must have defended you?"

"She tried, but she fell apart on the stand. Her words were taken out of context. She got confused. It was bad. In the end, I went to jail."

"It sounds so unfair."

"It felt that way to me."

She considered his words, and he was happy she hadn't rushed to judgment, although he couldn't imagine why she hadn't. Everyone else had been eager to form an immediate opinion.

"Did you mean to kill him?" she asked.

He shook his head. "I just wanted him to leave her alone. But I acted stupidly. It was a bad decision to confront him, one I've had plenty of time to think about."

"When did you get out?"

"Seven months ago. I've been trying to start over, but my old life is gone, and I haven't quite figured out where my new life is going."

"You have time."

"I guess." He fell silent as the phone on the desk rang again. This time—finally—the man in the Yankee cap strode forward to answer the call. "Looks like they're ready to deal," he murmured.

"Let's hope the cops are, too."

"Yeah?" the gunman said. After listening for a moment, he added, "You don't need to know my name." He paused again, his gaze moving toward Max. "He's fine, barely injured."

Spencer's lips tightened. Obviously, the police knew Max was hurt. They must have been able to regain some of the security video before the cameras were destroyed.

"No one is going anywhere," the gunman said. "We want a car at the door and two hundred thousand dollars in unmarked bills in a bag on the front seat." He listened again. "No one comes out until the car is here. I don't have to give you anything in return. You have fifteen minutes before we start killing hostages." He slammed the phone down without waiting for an answer.

"My brother doesn't have fifteen minutes," Spencer said to Hallie. He directed his next words to the gunmen. "You need to send out a hostage, show you're cooperating."

"We don't need your advice," the hooded man said.

"Look, you can let my brother go. I can carry him to the front door and put him outside. The paramedics can take him from there. He's no good to you. You can't use him as a shield. You can do that with me."

"Or me," Hallie put in. "I'll go with you."

"Hallie, no," Spencer said, but he could see the fighting light in her eyes.

"It doesn't matter if I die. I should be dead."

"Shut up—both of you," the hooded man replied. Then he and his partner moved away to talk again.

"They're not going for it," Spencer said. He looked into Hallie's gaze. "Thanks for the offer. That was brave."

She shrugged. "I just want to do something good for a change."

"You're doing that now. You're helping me save my brother's life."

"I hope so," she said. "If your hands are getting tired, we can switch."

"No, I'm good," he said, keeping the pressure on Max's abdomen. "Maybe the police will act quickly knowing that Max is hurt. Hopefully, it's five minutes instead of fifteen."

* * *

Emma couldn't stand the waiting. Every minute seemed like an eternity. After getting kicked out of the SWAT van, she'd been sidelined behind the police tape. Her father must have called her mother and siblings at some point, because her entire family and bridal party now surrounded her.

As she glanced over her shoulder at the group, it seemed a surreal site, a bridal party in gold gowns and black tuxedos gathered outside of a bank on a cold winter night. They were supposed to be at the reception now, drinking champagne and making toasts.

They were not supposed to be waiting out a hostage situation with Max's life in jeopardy. She could still see his body on the ground, blood spreading across his white shirt, Spencer rushing to his side and then some other woman coming over to help. Had they stopped the bleeding? Was the wound bad? She had a million questions and no answers.

She wrapped her arms around her waist and prayed for Max to make it through.

Burke came over to her side. "I just talked to Brady. They're making a deal. There should be some action soon."

"What kind of action?" she asked.

"I don't know."

"You do know, Burke, tell me." As a firefighter and arson investigator, she'd worked hostage situations before. She knew how delicate and dangerous the negotiation could be.

"They're going to get them a car and some cash," he said, compassion in his eyes.

Out of all of her family members, Burke probably came the closest to understanding her feelings right now. He'd lost his fiancé in a car crash just a few weeks before they were supposed to get married.

"Are they really going to let them walk out and drive away?" She didn't believe that for a second. "They're going to at least try to take a hostage with them."

"That won't be a man who's injured. Max won't be their shield."

"You're right. I just want this to be over."

"I'll see if I can find anything else out."

As Burke walked away, she returned her gaze to the bank. She'd gone to this branch a million times. She knew some of the tellers by sight. And nothing bad had ever happened. Why today?

"Em?"

She turned her head at the tentative voice and for some reason the sight of her brother Sean's face put tears in her eyes. He'd made it. And maybe because he'd made it, Max would, too. It was a completely irrational and illogical thought, but she grabbed on to it anyway.

He opened his arms, and she gave him a hug. "I'm so glad you're here."

"Sorry I'm late. I should have left a day earlier, given myself more time. I don't know why I didn't."

She knew why he'd put off the trip, because Sean was uncomfortable at family events. He was the lone ranger, the one Callaway who didn't fit in, the black sheep, at least in his mind, and probably her father's, too. Sean and her father had been at odds for as long as she could remember. In fact, sometimes she thought there was something more between them, something so deep and so private that only the two of them knew what it was. But whatever it was that stood between them, she hoped someday it would disappear, because she missed Sean being in her life.

"I'm just glad you're here now," she said. "Max was shot. I don't know how bad it is, but I don't think it's good."

"He's tough. Max will fight his way back to you, Em."

"I know he's trying."

"What can I do for you, Em? You need anything?"

"Just Max."

Sean nodded. "Do you want me to go? Nicole said you didn't want to talk to anyone."

"I don't want to talk, but I wouldn't mind the company," she said, knowing that Sean could stand quietly by her side and not say a word.

"You've got it."

They stood in silence for a few minutes and then Emma found a need to break the silence. "I'm going crazy. Tell me something to distract me. Tell me about your band."

"It's good. We just finished a three week tour through the Pacific Northwest."

"Where are you going next?" she asked.

"Nowhere. I'm going to be in San Francisco for a while. We're spending the next few weeks in the studio."

"That's great."

"Maybe," he said, doubt in his voice.

"What? You don't want to be home?" As she looked at him, she saw his gaze dart across the crowd to the woman standing close to Nicole. It was Jessica Schilling, the mother of Brandon's twin brother, Kyle. Nicole had told her that she thought there were sparks between Sean and Jessica, but Nicole had not wanted to encourage that connection. Jessica was practically one of the family now, and Sean didn't have a track record for long-term relationships. Nicole didn't want Sean to break Jessica's heart and cause a rift between Jessica and the Callaways, which, in turn, could hurt Brandon and Kyle's relationship.

As Sean didn't answer, she prodded, "Sean?"

He finally looked back at her. "What was the question?"

"Why don't you want to be home?"

"It's complicated."

"Is it Dad who complicates things? Or someone else?"

He smiled. "You're always so curious, Em."

Before she could press for more information, the police moved some cones to allow a car to drive past the barriers. The sedan stopped just a few feet from the front door. "Something's happening," she murmured, her heart jumping into overdrive.

Sean put his arm around her shoulder. She appreciated the warmth, because she was shaking with nervous chills.

She prayed to God that Max would be the first one out.

Chapter Seven

Max groaned, his eyelids fluttering.

"He's waking up," Spencer murmured, excitement in his voice.

While Hallie appreciated the fact that Max was regaining consciousness, she didn't want him moving. She put her hand around Max's cold fingers and said, "Stay still. Everything is okay. Don't move." Max seemed to settle a bit at her words. She looked back at Spencer. "We need to keep him quiet—for a lot of reasons."

Understanding flashed in Spencer's eyes. He knew as well as she did that besides the medical implications of Max awakening, jostling his wound and restarting the bleeding, it was better for all of them if Max remained still and didn't factor into any actions the robbers were considering. They were probably lucky that the gunmen had never looked at their I.D.'s, never realized Max was a cop. If they had, they'd probably be even more panicked than they already were.

She looked across the bank, watching the men pace and argue and then take a quick break to check the window. It was clear that they weren't in agreement about their next step or who was in charge. The hooded man seemed to be the most unpredictable. He was the one who'd shot Max without a second thought. The guy in the Yankee cap seemed more reasonable, but he was also getting worried. And why wouldn't he be? She couldn't imagine that the cops were going to let them walk out of the bank and drive away.

Max stirred again, his fingers twitching under her hand. He stretched one of his legs and then grimaced in pain. She put her other hand on Max's shoulder and leaned down next to his ear. "Don't move, Max. We need to get you back to..." She paused, looking at Spencer. "What's her name? The bride?"

"Emma."

She leaned back down. "We need to get you back to Emma, Max, but you have to stay still, so you don't start bleeding again."

His lips parted. "Emma," he breathed. "Love—love you."

Hallie's heart tore a little at his words. He thought she was Emma.

"Don't forget," he murmured.

"He thinks you're Emma," Spencer said.

"Then I'll be her." She squeezed Max's hand and said, "You have to fight, Max." She took a deep breath, not sure she could say the words she needed to say for Max, for Emma, because she hadn't said those words since her fiancé had died. In fact, her greatest regret was that she hadn't had a chance to say those words to Doug before he passed away. That night they'd been bickering a little, nothing serious, just the things couples do. What a waste of conversation and time that had been. How she wished she could have those moments back.

She couldn't change the past for herself or for Doug, but maybe the words could mean something now, to another man who really needed to hear them. She put her face right next to Max's. He was so weak, she could barely hear his breath. She needed to give him some strength.

"I love you," she whispered. "And I need you to come back to me. You have to stay still and rest, so the bleeding doesn't start again. You can do this, Max. Don't quit on me. We're not over yet. We're getting married, and we're having a future."

She sat back on her heels, hoping he'd heard her, hoping that he could hang on for the woman he loved. While she'd seen a lot of people die, she'd also seen a few miracles, and she wanted one for this man.

"Thanks," Spencer said.

"I hope it helped. I don't know what Emma would have said."

"Exactly what you did. He's calmer now."

"I hope he stays that way." She tucked a strand of her hair behind one ear as she looked out across the bank. "I wish these guys would calm down. The longer this goes on, the more nervous they get, and that makes them more dangerous. I thought this would be over by now." She could feel the tension rising in her own body. She needed to calm down, too.

"Tell me about the island you're going to," Spencer said.

"I don't know."

"You do know. Concentrate on that, Hallie."

She tried to focus on the dreamy image of paradise that had been getting her through the last few weeks.

"Are there palm trees?" he asked.

She nodded.

"Wide beaches?"

"With sand so hot it burns your toes," she said slowly.

"Good. What else?"

"The sea is blue-green, and the fish are so colorful, snorkeling is like looking through a kaleidoscope."

"Let's not forget about the rum," he said with a small smile.

"They put those little umbrellas in the drinks. And they have hammocks strung up between the trees where you can nap." She paused. "I think I might be able to sleep there. It will be quiet, no noises to wake me up and make me want to dive for cover. The only sound will be the waves crashing on the beach. But I've already missed my flight."

"You'll catch another one."

She nodded, realizing her pulse had slowed back down. "Thanks. I was getting wound up."

"You're doing great, Hallie. And when we get out of here, I'm going to buy you a rum drink with one of those umbrellas. I know a place right here in the city that makes them. It won't be your island bar, but it will tide you over until you can get there. What do you say?"

"That this is a first."

He sent her an enquiring look. "What do you mean?"

"It's the first time I've been asked out while I was trying to save someone's life and my own."

"I wasn't asking; I was telling," he said, a cocky note in his voice. "We're getting out of this, Hallie. And I'm going to buy you that drink. You can bet on that."

She liked his confidence. "You're on."

As she finished speaking, the phone rang again and the Yankee-capped man strode to the desk to answer it. He listened, then hung up and turned to his partner. "The car is here and the money. We're good to go."

"That's it? It seems too easy."

"I was just thinking that." Yankee set down his gun on the desk and walked to the window. "There are a million cops out there, probably snipers on the roof."

"I don't like it," the hooded man said. "They're setting us up."

"What do you want to do then? We can't stay in here all night."

Hallie sighed as their debate began again. At this point, any action was preferable to no action, especially where Max was concerned. His momentary calm had passed, and he was starting to move his legs now. He was also trying to pull his hand out of hers. She tightened her grip, then looked at Spencer.

"We have to do something," he said grimly.

She nodded. "The bleeding is starting up again, and he can't lose any more blood." She licked her lips, unable to believe what she was about to suggest. "I think we have to make a move."

He stared back at her. "I agree."

"You do?"

"Yes. We can wait it out, but Max can't. You're going to have to take over here, so I can try to get a jump on one of them."

"I can help. I'm a soldier. I know how to fight, Spencer."

"Not like this."

"Close enough," she said, remembering all the hand-to-hand combat training she'd undergone. It had been a long time, but she could do it. "You take one; I take the other. I think we can do it." She actually had no idea if they could do it or if they were about to commit suicide, but she didn't want to see Max die right in front of her without trying everything she could to save him.

His lips tightened. "We're only going to have one chance, one moment of surprise."

"The guy in the baseball cap put his gun on the desk," she said, meeting his gaze. "Now is the time."

"All right," he said decisively. "Start screaming. Pretend Max is dying, and you're terrified. Get hysterical on them. It will draw them over."

"Then what?"

"I'll jump the closest guy."

"Or I will."

"They could shoot you, Hallie."

She knew that was a real possibility but she was tired of being a victim. "I'll take the risk."

"All right. Ready?"

"More than ready." She drew in a breath and then started screaming. "Oh, my God, oh my God!" She put her hands on Max's chest as if she were searching for a heartbeat. "He's not breathing anymore. He's dying. Help! Help!" She jumped to her feet.

"What's going on?" the hooded gunman demanded, running over to them.

"We have to get him out of here," she yelled, waving her hand at Max. "Look, he's not breathing anymore. I have to get help. I can't let him die." She jerked to the right, and the gunman instinctively reached for her left arm. It was exactly what she wanted. She brought her other fist down hard on the back of his hand, the hand that was holding the gun.

He swore and dropped his weapon. It skidded across the floor. As he made a move to retrieve it, she kicked in the groin. He doubled over in pain.

Spencer leapt up and grabbed the gun off the floor. He was ready when the second man raced towards them, and he wasted no time pulling the trigger.

A split second later, a blast echoed through the bank.

Hallie saw the second gunman falter, but she didn't have time to see what happened next as the hooded man punched her in the nose. She fell backwards, clipping the side of a desk with her head as she fell toward the ground. She put up her hands to defend herself from the next attack, but it didn't come.

Spencer pulled the man off of her and hit him once, twice, a third time. The man retaliated, landing a blow on Spencer's jaw. They pummeled each other with desperate fury, a fight to the death.

Hallie tried to get up. She needed to help, but she was having trouble standing up. Stars were still exploding in front of her eyes. She forced herself to focus. She couldn't get to her feet, but she could crawl. She might not be able to help Spencer, but she could help Max. She got back to his side and put her hands on his bleeding wound.

And then the front door of the bank blasted open, the glass shattering into a million pieces, as the SWAT team rushed into the building. From there it was a flurry of action, the cops pulling Spencer and the gunman apart, the other hostages crying out with relief that it was finally over.

The paramedics rushed to her side, and she lifted her bloody hands off of Max as they went to work on him. Spencer came over as they hooked Max up to an IV and put him on a gurney.

"Where are you taking him?" Spencer asked.

"St. Mary's."

As the paramedics took Max out of the bank, Spencer turned to her. "We did it."

"Yeah," she said, wiping her hands on her jeans.

"Your nose is bleeding, Hallie."

"Is it?" She had so much blood on her hands and clothes, she didn't know where it was coming from. Spencer grabbed some tissue off a nearby desk and handed it to her. She pressed a wad of Kleenex to her nose. It hurt. She had a feeling it might be broken. But if that were the worst of it, she'd be happy. "Is the other guy dead?" she asked, looking at a second set of paramedics, who were working on the gunman Spencer had shot.

"No. I hit him in the leg."

"Nice shooting."

"It was instinct. You did the hard part, Hallie. You were amazing. So fearless."

"I wasn't fearless; I was terrified. But I knew that it was going to be him or us, so I did what I had to do."

"Yes, you did. You're stronger than you think."

"Maybe I am," she murmured.

"You need to go to the hospital, Hallie. Your nose could be broken, and your forehead is swelling up. You must be in pain."

"I'm not feeling anything right now."

"You will." Spencer called one of the cops over and told him she needed transportation to the hospital. She would have argued, because an emergency room was the last place she wanted to go, but she was feeling a little dizzy, and it probably wouldn't hurt to get checked out.

Before she left, she gave Spencer one last look. "You told me earlier that your brother was the good one. You're not so bad yourself."

"Right back at you," he said with a smile.

"Goodbye, Spencer."

"Not goodbye. I'll see you later. I still owe you that drink."

* * *

"Max," Emma screamed, as the paramedics exited the bank with Max strapped on to a stretcher.

She'd been holding her breath since the shots had gone off and the police had swarmed the bank. Her father and Sean had had to hold her back from rushing the scene. Now she broke free of their grip and sprinted across the street. She met up with Max at the door to the ambulance. His shirt was soaked in blood, and his face was terribly white. She put her hand on his. His skin was ice cold. He was so still, she couldn't even tell if he was breathing, if his heart was beating.

"I want to go with him," she told the paramedic.

"No. Sorry. Meet us at St. Mary's."

"Wait." She leaned over and gave him a quick kiss on the lips. "Fight, Max," she said.

And then the paramedics loaded him into the ambulance and closed the doors. As the vehicle raced away, she wished she'd had another second to tell Max how much she loved him, because she was very afraid she was not going to get another chance.

A fear like no other ran through her. She couldn't lose him now, before they'd even really started. She wanted years with him, marriage, children, and grandchildren.

She started to sway, and her father's arm came around her shoulders. She turned into his embrace, pressing her face against his chest. He patted her on the back. "It's going to be all right, Emma. Have faith."

She lifted her head to face him, needing the Jack Callaway power of conviction. When her father wanted something to happen, it happened.

"Max is a strong man," he told her. "And he needs you to believe in him."

"I do believe in him. But he's really hurt. I can't

believe this is happening. This was supposed to be the happiest day of my life."

"The day is not over yet. You are not a quitter, Emma. Lord knows you've proven that to me on a lot of occasions. Don't you give up on me now."

She drew in a deep breath. "I won't. You're right. Max is going to be fine, and one day this is just going to be a crazy story we tell our kids."

"That's my girl."

"Will you take me to the hospital?"

Her father nodded, but as they turned to leave, she stopped, looking back at the bank. "Where is Spencer? I should find him, make sure he's okay."

"Spencer is talking to Brady. You'll see him at the hospital. He's all right."

"Was he hurt?"

"No, from what I understand Max was the only one shot. Spencer actually took down the bank robbers and saved Max's life. He's a hero."

"Well, good for him," she said. "Max will be proud. He has tried to tell Spencer so many times that he is much more than just an ex-con. But Spencer hasn't been able to see that. Maybe he will now.

Chapter Eight

Ten minutes later, Emma and the rest of the Callaway clan, as well as Max's mother, Susan Harrison, gathered in the waiting room of the Emergency Department at St. Mary's Hospital. Information was not long in coming, but the news wasn't good.

"Mr. Harrison is being prepped for surgery," the attending physician told Emma. "He took a gunshot wound to the abdomen and suffered heavy blood loss. We won't know the extent of the internal damage until we operate."

"Oh, God!" Susan Harrison said, tears gathering in her eyes.

Emma took Max's mother's hand in hers. Then she turned back to the doctor and asked what they all wanted to know. "Is he going to be all right?"

"We're doing everything we can. The nurse will take you up to the third floor and show you where you can wait." He tipped his head to the woman in blue scrubs standing nearby. "Mr. Harrison will be in surgery for several hours. The surgeon will be Dr. Blake Holland. He will speak to you as soon as it's done."

As the E.R. physician left, Emma looked at the nurse. "He didn't really answer my question."

The nurse gave her a compassionate smile. "Let me show you to the waiting room."

"You're not going to answer my question, either, are you?"

"I'm afraid I don't know the answer, but I can tell you that Dr. Holland is the best surgeon we have. Mr. Harrison is in good hands." She turned and headed toward the elevator.

"The doctor is one of the best," Emma told Susan, as they followed the nurse down the hall. Her words didn't seem to register. Max's mother was terrified, which only made Emma more worried. A part of her wanted to get away from the older woman's negativity, but she knew that Max would want her to make sure that his mother was all right.

"I can't lose Max," Susan said. "He's always taken care of me, even though I drive him crazy half the time."

"We're not going to lose him. I have big plans for your son." As they neared the elevator, Susan hesitated. "Maybe I should wait here for Spencer."

"They'll tell him where to find us," Emma replied.

"I can't believe my boys got caught up in a bank robbery. I blame myself for that."

"Why?" she asked in surprise.

"Because I suggested Max change his money before going to the airport."

"You had no way of knowing what would happen."

"I didn't. But I really wish I hadn't said that." She paused. "Max was so happy this afternoon. When he came by to get Spencer, he had the biggest smile on his face. It was blinding. I hadn't seen him like that in such a long time. It reminded me of the way he was as a little boy, so eager, curious, and optimistic. That all changed when his father left us. Max lost his joy. But he got it back when he met you." She gave Emma a sad smile. "You changed his life."

"He changed mine, too," Emma said, as they stepped onto the elevator. "And I'm not giving up. You shouldn't, either. Max would want us to be strong."

"He would," Susan agreed. "And I'm rarely as strong as my son would like me to be. But you are. You're going to get him through this."

"We both are."

Stepping off the elevator, they entered a nearby waiting room. Emma took a seat in a chair against the wall, happy when her mother made a point of asking Susan to sit with her, so Emma could have some time to herself. The rest of her family and bridal party spread out, smaller groups forming here and there. The cops and firefighters had stayed downstairs, so as not to crowd the family, but Emma knew there was a lot of support a few floors down.

Nicole sat down next to her. "Can I get you anything, Em? Coffee? Water? Food? It sounds like we're going to be here for awhile."

"I don't want anything."

As she shifted in her seat, her gaze caught on a splash of red on the waist of her wedding dress. Her heart skipped a beat. She must have gotten the blood on her dress when she'd leaned over to kiss Max. She put her fingers against the red stain and then her mouth started to tremble. She had to bite down on her bottom lip to stop the cry of pain from slipping past her lips.

"Emma?" Nicole asked, her brows knitting together with concern.

"This is Max's blood. He lost so much."

"If he needs blood, he'll get it. We'll line up the family, the firefighters and the police officers, and there will be plenty of blood flowing his way. And don't be thinking it's too late, because it's not. Callaways don't quit, and we don't give up."

"You sound like Dad," she said with a sniff.

"I was channeling him just now," Nicole admitted. "But the important thing is that he's right."

"I know."

"I need to check in with Jessica, see how Brandon is doing, but I'll be right back."

"That's fine." As Nicole left, Emma settled back in her chair and rested her head against the wall. Closing her eyes, she said a silent prayer for Max's recovery. He had to get better, because he was truly the love of her lifetime. She forced the image of him lying so still, covered in blood, out of her mind and tried to bring up the happy memories.

They'd had a lot of good moments in the past year, but probably the best was the day they'd moved into their apartment.

She smiled to herself as she drifted to a happier place…

It was after midnight.

They'd spent the night unpacking boxes and arguing about where to put the ugly recliner Max thought was perfect for watching ballgames, and she thought was perfect for the dumpster.

Max had ended up winning the argument with a kiss that had turned into much, much more. After making love, they'd been lying on the floor of their barely furnished apartment when Max rolled over on to his side and gave her a serious look.

"What?" she asked. "If you thought making love to me was going to make me change my mind about the recliner, you do not know me at all. I am not that easy." She smiled, then started to worry when his expression only grew more serious. "Okay, I am that easy. If you really want the recliner—"

"Emma, I don't give a damn about the recliner."

"Then why do you look so concerned? What are you worrying about?"

"Whether or not you'll say yes, or if you'll think it's soon, too fast."

Her heart started to beat in triple time. "Yes to what, Max?"

He gave her a long look. "Will you marry me, Em?"

The question took her breath away. She hadn't been expecting him to propose so soon after moving in together. She'd thought they were easing their way towards a more permanent commitment.

"Okay, now I'm thinking it is too soon," he said when she didn't answer. "Sorry, forget I asked."

She immediately shook her head. "No, it's the perfect time—for the question and for the answer. Which is yes. I love you, Max. I want to marry you. I want to have a life with you."

Relief flooded his eyes. "I love you, too, Emma. You are the most stubbornly annoying, beautiful, generous, smart woman, I know."

"Hey, you could leave out a few of those adjectives," she protested. "And I'm not the only one who's stubborn. You have a very hard head."

He smiled. "I know. We're a perfect match. I want to live with you and love you and fight with you every day of our lives."

"Maybe we can keep the fights to only every now and

then," she teased. "Or maybe never if you agree to put that chair in the dumpster."

"Fine, the chair goes in the dumpster."

"I was just kidding. If you can't live without it, then it stays. And I'll be very happy to curl up on your lap while you're sitting in it."

"The only thing I can't live without is you."

"You don't have to. I'm not going anywhere."

"Good."

"So when did you decide you wanted to marry me?" she asked.

"After our first fight."

"We fought the first day we met," she reminded him. "We were working on a case and you didn't want to share your information with me."

"And you didn't want to share your info with me, either. But I thought you were gorgeous with your silky blond hair and spitfire blue eyes."

"I thought you were annoying, but also kind of hot," she admitted.

"I liked that you didn't back down."

"No, you didn't," she teased.

"Okay, maybe I didn't like it that much. But I know that life with you is going to be one hell of a ride."

"Never boring. So when do you want to get married?"

"Whenever you want. But for now..." He got up and walked across the room, pulling a jewelry box out of his coat pocket. Then he came back to her. "I was going to give this to you tomorrow, on your birthday." He glanced at the clock. "Actually it's after midnight, so it is your birthday." He opened the lid. "What do you think?"

She gasped at the sight of beautiful square-cut diamond ring. "It's gorgeous. And it's so me. You did good."

"I had a little help from your sister, Nicole. Do you like it?"

"I love it."

He slipped it on to her finger. "It fits."

"It does," she said, tears blurring her eyes as she looked from the ring to him. "You just have to make me one promise, Max."

"Anything."

"Don't ever leave me."

"I promise," he said, then kissed away her tears. "You and I are going to be together for a very long time."

The memory of Max's words echoed through Emma's head as the dream faded away. She opened her eyes and looked around the waiting room, wishing she could go back to the happy place. But reality was right in front of her.

There were a lot of concerned faces turned in her direction, but everyone was giving her space. Her family knew her well. She was a strong person, and she knew how to fight, but sometimes she needed to be in her head for a few minutes so she could get past the fear and get onto the battle ahead.

She straightened in her chair as Spencer entered the room. His tuxedo jacket was missing. His white shirt and gold tie were covered in blood. His face looked battered, a golf-ball sized swelling around his right eye that was turning a dark shade of purple. His mother ran to him, giving him a long, tight hug.

"I'm okay, Mom," he said.

"You're hurt?"

"It's not a big deal," he said, gently extricating himself from her embrace. He walked over to Emma. "I'm so sorry."

"It's not your fault," she said, getting up to give him a

hug. "And from what I hear, you were quite the hero."

"When will we know anything?"

"The doctor said it could be a few hours. Can you tell me what happened, Spencer?"

"Sure," he said, waving her back into her chair. Then he sat down next to her. "What do you want to know?"

"Everything. Your mom said Max went to the bank to change some money?"

"For your honeymoon. It was supposed to be a quick, ten-minute stop." Spencer shook his head, his lips tightening. "And then it all went to hell."

"How did Max get shot?"

"One of the bank employees went to hit the silent alarm on her computer. The gunman saw her and just as he pulled the trigger, Max dived in front of her. He was acting the hero—as usual. I told him not to, but does he ever listen to me?" he said gruffly.

She heard the pain in Spencer's voice. He was covering up his fear with anger. "What happened next?"

"I tried to stop the bleeding, but I didn't know what I was doing. Fortunately, there was a nurse in the bank, Hallie Cooper. She told me what to do."

"Thank God. Was Max in a lot of pain? Was he talking?"

Spencer hesitated.

"What did he say?" she pressed.

"He wanted me to tell you that he loved you, Emma."

She put a hand to her mouth, tears welling up again. "He didn't think he was going to make it, did he?"

"You were on his mind. You're always on his mind. My brother is crazy about you." He paused. "After that, he passed out. It was better that way. His body was resting. But then, towards the end, he started to get restless. I had trouble keeping pressure on the wound. Hallie and I realized that we were running out of time. The gunmen didn't know what to do. They were afraid they were going to get shot walking out the door."

"So what did you do?" she asked, a shiver running down her spine as his words took her right into the bank, into the terrifying ordeal.

"One of the men had left his gun on the desk by the phone when he went to look out the window. It was our chance to make a move. Hallie started screaming, telling the other guy that Max was dying. When he came close, she knocked the gun out of his hand. I picked up his gun and shot the other guy. It all happened really fast. Looking back, I wish we'd acted sooner. But we kept thinking it was going to be over in a minute."

"You took the only opportunity you had, Spencer. And Hallie sounds incredibly brave."

"She was amazing," he said, admiration in his tone. "She's downstairs getting checked out. That guy might have broken her nose. I need to go check on her."

"I'll go with you."

"Really? You don't want to wait here?"

"I could use a walk, and I want to meet her—thank her."

"You can do that later."

"The surgery is going to take hours, and I've never been good at waiting." She got to her feet and turned to her mother. "Spencer and I are going to check on the woman who helped saved Max. I'll just be a few minutes, but you'll come find me if there's any news?"

"I will," Lynda promised.

As they walked out of the waiting room, Emma said, "Did Max tell you where he was taking me on our honeymoon?"

Spencer hesitated. "He did, but I can't tell you,

Emma."

"Why not?"

"Because Max wants it to be a surprise."

She met his gaze and appreciated what he wasn't saying. "You're right. I'll let him tell me himself. Or better yet—show me."

Chapter Nine

Hallie winced as the E.R. doctor finished his examination of her bruised nose.

"I don't think it's broken," he said. "The swelling should go down within twenty-four hours. You're going to have some nice shiners though."

"Great. Raccoon eyes. I can't wait."

"As for your head, the CT scan was normal, but you should take it easy for the next day or two. I'll give you a prescription for some painkillers, and you can be on your way."

She was relieved to hear that. Being back in a hospital felt both awkward and strangely comfortable. For the past ten years, her life had revolved around medicine. Hospitals had been her second home. All of her friends had been doctors and nurses, lab techs and orderlies. And when she'd gone into the Army, the uniforms had changed but not the medicine.

She'd always been good at her job. It was the one

place where she'd felt smart, proud and in control—until her life and her love had blown up right in front of her. She forced the image out of her mind, but she knew the memories would always be there lurking in the background, bringing stress and anxiety to every day of her life.

"You should continue to ice. It will help the bruising," the doctor added.

"I'm a nurse. I know what to do."

"Sometimes nurses make the worse patients."

"I think they say that about doctors."

He smiled. "Probably true. Call me if you have any unexpected pain or severe bleeding."

"I will."

As the doctor left the room, Spencer walked in, followed by a blond woman wearing an overcoat over a wedding gown. Hallie knew immediately who she was. This was Max's bride—

Emma.

"Hallie, how are you?" Spencer asked, concern in his eyes. "Is your nose broken?"

"No, just bruised. How did you know where I was?"

"Emma got it out of the nurse. She was quite persistent." He smiled at the bride. "Emma, this is Hallie Cooper—Emma Callaway."

Emma walked over to the examining table, her blue eyes showing strain and gratitude.

"I want to thank you, Hallie. Spencer told me what you did for Max. I'm sorry you were caught up in such a bad situation, but I'm also really glad you were there." She frowned. "That sounds bad—"

"I know what you mean," Hallie said, cutting her off. "And I was happy to help. Max said your name a few times and told us he loved you."

Emma's eyes began to water. "I didn't think he was conscious."

"He drifted in and out," Hallie said. "But it was clear he was thinking about you." She hoped her words were making Emma feel better, but as a tear slid out of the corner of her eye, she thought maybe not.

Emma wiped the tear away. "I'm not going to cry," she said. "Max will be all right. He's tough."

"Max is in surgery now," Spencer put in.

"That's good." She paused. "I appreciate you coming to check on me, but you should go back to your families."

"I think I will do that," Emma said.

"I'll be up in a minute," Spencer said.

"Okay." Emma smiled at Hallie. "I hope you feel better. I know Max is going to want to meet you when he wakes up."

"I would love to see him back on his feet."

As Emma left the room, Hallie swallowed a little nervously. She was suddenly aware of Spencer in a very different way. They'd been caught up in a life and death situation, no time to think, only to act, and they'd bonded, connected on a level that only an extremely dangerous moment could bring on. But that moment was over. Now what?

Now—nothing, she told herself. She'd made a plan for her life, a plan to lie on a beach for a few months and regroup. She might have missed her flight, but there would be another one tomorrow. She should be on it.

"What a day, huh?" Spencer asked, folding his arms in front of his chest. "It feels surreal. Like a dream."

"More like a nightmare. Did you talk to the police?"

"Yeah, that's why it took me so long to get here."

"What happened to the gunmen?"

"The one I shot was taken to another hospital. The

other one is being booked into jail. They're going to go away for a long time."

"I hope so."

"Have you talked to police?" Spencer asked.

"I spoke to someone when I first got here. He brought me my phone, my wallet, and my now worthless plane ticket. He said he'd call me tomorrow if he had any other questions, but I'm sure all of us will tell the same story." She slid off the table, feeling a little steadier now. The dizzying adrenaline had finally worn off.

"Are you sure you're okay?" Spencer asked.

"I am sure. And I'd like to get out of here."

"How are you getting home?"

"Good question. My car is still at the bank. I guess I'll take a cab and get it tomorrow. Although, it will be weird to go back there."

"Take someone with you."

"I can handle it."

"I'm sure you can," he said with a smile. "Why don't you call a family member now to take you home?"

It was a simple question, but she didn't have a simple answer. "I don't have anyone to call."

His gaze narrowed speculatively. "No family?"

"I don't have anyone to call," she repeated, hoping he'd let it end there.

Of course he didn't. "Why not? Where are they?" he asked.

She sighed. "You don't let things go, do you?"

"I'm curious."

"Fine. My father lives in the East Bay, but we haven't spoken to each other in a few months."

"Why not?"

"He didn't like something I did," she replied.

"What about your mother?"

"She died when I was ten. And my only brother is overseas, if that's your next question. He's an Air Force pilot."

"Did your father serve in the military as well?"

"For many years," she said. "Are you done?"

He gave her a small smile. "I'm just getting started. If you're not in a rush to get home, can I buy you a cup of coffee in the cafeteria?"

She should say no. She should end this relationship— or whatever it was—now, before anything else happened. She was broken, and her life was a mess, and the last thing she needed to do was involve anyone else in it. But there was something about Spencer that called out to her. So instead of turning him down, she said. "All right. I don't need any caffeine though. Maybe some herbal tea." As they walked out of the exam room, she added. "Are you sure you don't want to get back to your family?"

"My mother is being soothed by Mrs. Callaway, and I could use a moment to catch my breath. There are going to be a lot of questions, and I'm not ready to answer them all yet."

She could understand that. "Then let's get some tea."

* * *

The hospital cafeteria was located in the basement and it was relatively empty, which wasn't surprising for nine o'clock on a Saturday night. Hallie couldn't believe that so much had happened in just a few hours. While Spencer went for decaf coffee, Hallie poured a cup of hot tea, and they sat down at a table in the corner.

As Spencer sipped his coffee, she let herself really look at him. When he'd first flirted with her in line, she'd been so focused on getting out of town and running away from her life, that she hadn't wanted to acknowledge how handsome he was, or the little flutter of attraction that had run through her when their eyes had met. In fact, she'd try to tell herself that flutter was indigestion, because there was no way she could feel anything for a man ever again. She was numb inside. Her soul had died.

But she was wrong about not being able to feel something. In fact, the nervous flutter was back, and it had nothing to do with indigestion, and everything to do with the tall, handsome, dark-haired man in front of her.

"You're staring," Spencer said.

She started as he lifted his gaze to meet hers. "Sorry. I was looking at your bruises. Nurse's habit," she lied. She didn't want him to think she was interested in him, because nothing was going to happen. How crazy would she be to get involved with a man she barely knew? And what she did know was a little alarming. He'd killed a man. He'd gone to prison. It sounded like a raw deal, but she'd only heard one side of the story.

On the other hand, actions spoke louder than words, and she'd seen Spencer in action. He'd been thoughtful and smart, staying calm when she'd been extremely anxious. And he'd fought for his brother and for her. He had demonstrated great courage, and she would always be grateful to him. But they were sitting here having tea and coffee because of gratitude. They both knew that.

"You said you weren't a nurse anymore," Spencer reminded her. "So my bruises shouldn't concern you."

"Some habits don't go away. You should put some ice on your face."

"I could say the same to you."

At his remark, she found herself smiling. "We must make a great looking couple."

He smiled back at her. "It's probably good we don't

have a mirror."

"I wondered why the cashier gave us such a wary look. She probably thought we beat each other up."

"How's your tea?"

"Warm and soothing. I feel better."

"Good. You've probably spent a lot of time in hospital cafeterias."

"More time than in my own kitchen."

He rested his forearms on the table as he leaned forward, giving her an interested look. "Tell me your story, Hallie."

"I already told you when we were in the bank," she prevaricated.

"You said your fiancé was killed, but not why you quit nursing."

She shook her head. "I don't want to do this."

"Do what?"

"Exchange life stories. Pretend we're friends."

"How could we not be friends after everything we went through together?"

"But we're never going to see each other again after tonight."

"Of course we are. I still owe you a rum drink. You promised to let me buy you one."

"Then we won't see each other again after that."

"Hallie. Just talk to me. That's all I'm asking."

She slid her finger around the rim of her teacup. "That's asking a lot. A lot of bad things happened."

"And you're keeping them all inside."

"Why torture anyone else?" she asked.

"When it's so much easier to just torture yourself," he finished.

"Maybe I deserve it."

"I won't know until you talk to me." He paused.

"When I went to prison, I was filled with rage at the injustice of what had happened to me. I couldn't talk to anyone about it, because I was so angry. I blamed the people around me for not doing enough. Max was a big target. I refused to see him after the first few visits. And after that, he stopped trying to see me. Most everyone else did, too. I had no one to talk to, because that's the way I wanted it, and I was as trapped in my head as I was trapped in that cell. Everything just festered inside of me. It was so bad I gave myself an ulcer. And I finally, finally realized that I wasn't punishing anyone else with my attitude, only myself. The anger was killing me more than the prison term."

"And you just let it go? Just like that?"

"God, no! Not just like that. It's still not completely gone, but I've done some talking the past few months. I've stopped making my world all about me about that one terrible event in my life. I'm starting to look out, instead of in." He paused. "I don't want to see you waste as much time as I did."

"Talking won't change anything."

"Maybe it will. Maybe you need to say something out loud and really hear the words. I'm not going to judge you, Hallie. I'm the last person who could judge anyone."

She stared back at him indecisively. She'd only told the whole story to one other person, her father, and he had judged her.

She tapped her fingers nervously on the tabletop, torn between a sudden desire to unload and a self-protective instinct to stay quiet. How could she trust Spencer, when the man who'd raised her, the man she adored and admired, had looked at her with disgust and disappointment? She was just setting herself up for another fall.

Spencer covered her nervous fingers with his warm hand, and his gaze met hers. "I promise, Hallie. You talk, I listen. No opinion."

She debated another minute and then said. "I'll start. I'm not sure how far I'll get."

"One step at a time."

She licked her lips. "We were in the middle East. My fiancé was a soldier. We'd been going out for almost a year and we'd gotten engaged just before Christmas, last year. Another reason why I really hate this season."

He nodded. "Go on."

"I asked Doug to meet me one night. I wanted to talk about our wedding plans. It was late, and he was tired. He'd been out all day that day, but I pushed him to meet me." She shook her head at the memory. "It was so stupid. My friend had sent me a bridal magazine, and I wanted to show him the dress I liked. As if it mattered to him what I wore. He didn't care at all about dresses or flowers or anything. He just wanted to marry me. I was getting too worked up about silly little things."

"What happened?"

She opened her mouth to answer, but instead of seeing Spencer's face in front of her, she saw blinding headlights. She heard the shouts to stop, and felt the terrifying fear of death run through her.

"Hallie."

Spencer's voice brought her back to the present.

"A truck came crashing through the gate," she said. "Not far from where we were standing. Doug instinctively moved towards the danger. That's the kind of man he was. A guy leaned out of the truck with an automatic weapon in his hand. He fired three times. Doug fell face down on the ground. I screamed. I started to go to him, and then the whole world exploded. I was thrown back ten feet."

Spencer squeezed her hand, his gaze filling with compassion. "You don't have to go on, Hallie. I'm sorry. I shouldn't have asked you to relive something that horrific."

"It's okay," she said, taking a moment to breathe. "I have to finish, because that's not where the story ends."

He stared back at her. "Where does it end?"

"On the operating table."

"You couldn't save Doug," he said flatly.

She shook her head. "I didn't have a chance to save Doug. After the explosion, he wasn't on the ground anymore. His body…Well, he never made it to the O.R." She couldn't go into any more detail than that.

His lips tightened. "So what happened on the table?"

"After the blast, there were a lot of injuries. I wanted to scream and cry and mourn for Doug, but there were other soldiers to save, and some of them were my friends. I went to work, and I put everything else out of my mind, the way I was trained to do." She paused, her mind going back in time again. "I was moving so fast. It was a blur of faces, bodies, blood—so much blood. And then I saw someone I recognized. It wasn't a soldier. It was the man in the truck, the one who'd shot Doug."

Spencer blew out a breath. "What did you do?"

"The doctor was giving me orders, but I couldn't hear him. I couldn't move. I looked at that man on the table, and I saw a murderer. All I could think was that this man was supposed to die. He wanted to die. He was a suicide bomber. Why should I save him?" She met Spencer's gaze head on. "You can probably guess what happened."

"He died," Spencer said.

She nodded. "It was my fault."

"Was it? Or were his injuries so severe that he couldn't be saved?" Spencer challenged.

"Some of my friends made that excuse for me," she

conceded. "But it didn't change what I'd done or didn't do. Medicine isn't supposed to be about right and wrong, good people and bad people. You're supposed to try to save the patient in front of you. That's all that matters, and I didn't do that. I didn't just freeze. I deliberately chose not to act. I went against everything I believed in, everything I was about." She took a breath. "I haven't been back in the operating room since that night. They sent me to counseling, and I told the psychiatrist I couldn't go back, and he eventually recommended discharge. Since I got out, I've been trying to decide what the hell I'm going to do with my life now. All I ever wanted to be was a nurse. I don't know how to do anything else."

"You were a nurse tonight. You saved Max's life."

"I hope I helped, but you did the hard part, Spencer."

"You told me what to do. And you talked to Max. You kept him quiet. You made him believe in Emma and their love."

"Instinct took over." She sipped her tea, feeling surprisingly better and a little lighter having told the whole story. Maybe she had needed to say it out loud. And Spencer hadn't judged her. There had been no disgust in his eyes, only kindness. "Thank you, Spencer. For doing what you said, offering no opinion about what I did, or didn't do. My father had a lot to say. And it was not good."

"Is that why you haven't spoken to him?"

"He's extremely disappointed in me, so yes."

"How could he not understand why you acted the way you did?"

"Because he's a brilliant doctor, and he would never walk away from a patient, no matter what they'd done."

"Maybe he's never been tested the way you were."

"I think he has. He's just stronger than me. He's really an incredible person. I've always loved him and admired him and wanted to be just like him. But I couldn't live up to his example. I fell really short."

"So you told him, and he said…"

"Nothing. He just stared at me. It was the longest silence of my life. Then I left. That was it. I don't blame him. I know what I did was wrong."

Spencer frowned. "You're being extremely hard on yourself, Hallie. You'd just seen your fiancé die. It's surprising you could do anything at all at that point."

"Don't let me off the hook."

"I couldn't do that if I tried. You're the only one who can do that. I don't know if what you did in that operating room was as horrible as you think it was. But I do know what you did today, and it was amazing. Just coming to my aid put you in danger, but you did it anyway. And then you take on a man with a gun twice your size? You were brave and selfless, and you should be proud of yourself."

Her eyes filled with tears, the intensity of his words breaking down the walls of guilt and shame she'd built up in her head. "You're being really nice, Spencer."

"You have to stop defining yourself by one moment in your past."

"Isn't that what you've been doing?"

"I'm trying to change. So should you. Because when I thought we might die in that bank, I realized how much I want to live."

"I had the same thought," she admitted. "I wanted to die for a long time. I kept asking why Doug, why not me? But when I saw death staring me in the face, I knew I didn't want that at all."

"And Doug wouldn't want it for you. He'd want you to make the most of your life."

"He would," she said, tearing up again. "You're right." He squeezed her fingers again, and she realized they were still holding hands, and she didn't want to let go. "We are quite a pair, aren't we?" she asked. "And I'm not talking about the bruises anymore."

"We've both been to hell. But we're not there anymore."

"What have you been doing since you got out of prison?" she asked, curious about who he was now.

"Working in a deli. It's a quite change from my old job as a commodities trader, but I couldn't do that anymore. And with a record, I couldn't be too choosey. Anyway, since being at the deli, I've been toying with the idea of becoming a chef.

"Really?" she asked in surprise.

"It's probably a crazy dream."

"But it's a great dream."

"I like to cook. I need to get better."

"So you'll get better. I hate to cook, but I really like to eat."

"Maybe you'll let me practice on you."

"Maybe." She paused as the staff began to close down the cafeteria. "I think it's time to go."

"Yeah." He let go of her hand. "I need to get upstairs anyway."

She nodded, feeling a little chill now that there was distance between them.

"Would you come with me?" he asked as they headed out the door.

She hesitated. "Oh, I don't know. You have your family and friends."

"But I want you."

His simple words sent a shiver down her spine.

And once again, when she should have said *no*, she found herself saying *yes*.

Chapter Ten

As they walked out of the cafeteria, Spencer stayed close to Hallie's side. It was strange and rather amazing the connection he felt to her. He'd felt closed off and numb for so long, but now his skin was tingling, and his black and white world was filling with color. He just needed Max to recover in order to really enjoy the new feelings of hope and optimism for the future.

They took the elevator to the third floor and walked down the hall to the waiting room. There at least twenty people inside, most of them Callaways, and many of whom he'd met the night before at the rehearsal dinner. That seemed like a lifetime ago.

"I should go," Hallie murmured, holding back when they reached the doorway. "I don't belong here."

"I don't, either," he said.

"You're his brother."

"And these are mostly his in-laws. I could use a friend."

"Fine, but stop telling everyone I saved Max's life. You're giving me too much credit."

He smiled. "And you're being way too modest. You don't have to meet everyone, but I do want to introduce you to my mother."

"Really?" she asked, doubt in her voice. "Your mom?"

"It won't hurt a bit," he said lightly.

"You know when nurses say that, they're lying," she told him.

He smiled and led her across the room to where his mother was sitting next to Emma's mom, Lynda. They both got up to hug him. And when they were done, he found himself the recipient of many more Callaway hugs. By the time he got through the family, he could see Hallie caught up in the same warm receiving line, as Emma told her family that this was the woman who saved Max's life. At least, Hallie couldn't blame him for the attention.

When they'd gone through the line, they took a seat against the far wall.

"Well," Hallie murmured. "That was crazy. Are these people always so welcoming?"

He nodded. "Yeah, pretty much. They already consider Max a friend, a son, a brother, and a brother-in-law."

"I hope you're not worried about losing him to the Callaways, because I think they're officially adopting you and your mother, too."

"They've been great," he agreed. "I'm happy for Max." As he settled into his seat, he saw her take out her phone and check the messages. "Anything important come in?"

"No, just an alert that I missed my flight."

"There's probably one tomorrow. You should check."

"I'll do it later," she said.

He was happy to see her put away her phone, because

the last thing he wanted her to do was get on a plane. "What do you usually do for Christmas, when you're not heading for the tropics?"

"I actually missed Christmas last year. I couldn't get home. But before that I always celebrated with my dad, and sometimes with my brother, if he could make it back. My Aunt Debbie, and her husband and kids, would come over on Christmas Eve. She was like a second mom to me after my mother died. We'd have a big dinner and exchange presents. Then on Christmas Day we always went to church in the morning and then had a big lunch after that. Sometimes we'd invite the neighbors in or some of my father's friends. It was different every year."

"It sounds nice," he said, hearing the wistful note in her voice. "Aren't you going to miss that?"

"I'd just put a damper on things."

"No one else besides your dad knows about…"

"They know about Doug, but nothing else, unless my father told Aunt Debbie, but I doubt he would do that."

"You've had no communication with him since the day you told him?"

She hesitated. "He's texted a few times."

"Really?" he asked, shifting in his seat. "You didn't mention that before. Did you text him back?"

"No."

"Hallie, what are you doing?"

"Hey, you said you weren't going to judge."

"I'm not judging, I'm asking you a question. Why haven't you responded to his texts?"

"I don't know."

"Yes, you do."

"Look, I had a plan to get out of town and take my problems with me. It was a good plan, until it all went to hell when I decided to stop at the bank."

"Maybe something good will come of today."

"Like what?"

"A chance to make things right. We both know life is short. You love your dad. You should talk to him again. Give it one more try. He deserves that, and so do you."

"Maybe. I'll think about it." She crossed her legs and folded her arms in front of her chest, as if she were settling in for the long haul, and they probably were.

He was glad Hallie had stayed for so many reasons, but one of the biggest was that he'd rather spend the waiting time getting to know her than thinking about how badly Max was hurt. He couldn't get the sight of all that blood out of his head, especially when his clothes were still covered in it. He just hoped the bullet had missed the vital organs and that they hadn't waited too long to act.

"Spencer?"

He met Hallie's gaze.

"Don't go back there," she said.

"Are you reading my mind now?"

"Max is in good hands. There's nothing to do but wait," she said.

"You're right."

"So what do you like to cook?" she asked.

"A lot of things."

"Like?"

"Well, I just made a really good curry dish with lamb."

"Sounds delicious. I love curry. Tell me more."

He gave her a doubtful look. "You really want to talk about food?"

"It seems like a good topic to me, and one that isn't going to upset either one of us."

"I might bore you to sleep."

She smiled. "I'll take that risk."

"You are the daredevil."

"Don't you know it," she said lightly.

He smiled back at her. "Okay, then let me tell you about this stew I'm working on…"

* * *

Emma glanced at the clock on the wall, feeling as if the minutes were passing with agonizing slowness. Max had been in surgery for almost four hours, and she was tired of waiting. Her siblings and parents had been great at trying to keep her distracted, but they'd eventually run out of things to say, and she'd drunk enough coffee to sink a ship, which probably hadn't been a good idea. The caffeine had only made her more jumpy and anxious.

Nicole came into the room after having gone to check with the nurse's station. She immediately shook her head at Emma's silent question. "No news yet, but they think it will be soon."

"They said that an hour ago."

"I know," Nicole said. "But let's go with no news is good news."

She saw the weariness in her sister's face. "If you need to go home, Nicole, I can call you—"

"Don't be silly. I'm not going anywhere. Jessica is keeping Brandon overnight, so I'm all yours."

Shayla came over to join them. "I talked to a friend of mine who's an intern here. He said he thinks the surgery is almost done. He also reiterated that Dr. Holland is brilliant."

Emma was happy to hear both of those statements.

"I never think about the people waiting," Shayla said, as she took a seat. "In medical school, we're so focused on the physical body, on diagnosis, treatment, pharmaceuticals, but we don't spent a lot of time thinking about the people in the waiting room. I'm going to remember this feeling when I'm a surgeon."

"You're going to make a really good one," Emma said. Shayla had always been an academic overachiever, but it was nice to see her taking in the whole picture.

She'd no sooner finished speaking than the door opened, and a doctor walked in. He was dressed in scrubs and booties and looked like he'd come straight from the O.R.

Emma jumped to her feet and rushed across the room. Susan was just as fast. They grabbed each other's hand as they faced the doctor together.

"I'm Dr. Holland," he said. "Mr. Harrison is doing well. He made it through the surgery without complications, and we're anticipating a full recovery."

It took a minute for his words to register through the fear. "Oh, my God," Emma said, putting her other hand to her heart. "Can you say that again?"

The doctor smiled. "He's going to be fine, but he'll need some recovery time."

She blew out a breath, feeling an enormous weight lift off her chest. "That is the best news. Thank you so much."

"Mr. Harrison did the hard work," the doctor said. "He's a fighter."

"I know," she replied, never doubting that Max would fight to come back to her. "When can I see him?"

"He'll be asleep for a few hours."

"I want to sit with him. Can I do that? Please."

He nodded. "Of course, but only one of you. We'll save the other visits for tomorrow afternoon."

Emma nodded her agreement.

"The nurse will come and get you when Mr. Harrison is back in his room."

As the doctor left, she looked around at her friends and family, the people who had stood by her on the worst day of her life. "He's going to be okay," she said again, happiness racing through her veins.

Her words were met with a chorus of cheers and smiles, all except for Max's mother, who was quietly weeping into her tissue.

"Susan," Emma said, squeezing her hand.

"Don't mind me," Susan said. "These are happy tears now." She gave Emma a watery smile. "My boy is going to be all right."

"He is." Emma hesitated. The last thing she wanted to do was give up her seat at Max's bedside, but she knew his mother was very worried about him, too. "Do you want to go in and see him first?"

"Oh, no, dear," she said, shaking her head. "Max will want you there, Emma. Just tell him we're all thinking about him."

"Spencer?" she asked, offering him the same courtesy.

He smiled. "Are you kidding? I'm not the pretty face my brother wants to see when he wakes up. But tell him next time he wants to go to the bank, I'm going to pass."

"Online banking from here on," she agreed. She looked back at her sister, Nicole. "We should make some calls, let people know."

"I'm on it," Nicole said. "I'll start with the guys downstairs."

"And I'll call the family," Lynda said.

"I'll go through the wedding list with Cynthia and make sure all the guests get an update," Shayla said. "Don't worry about anything, Emma. Just go see your man."

"I will. You've all been amazing to me. I couldn't have gotten through this without any you. I'm so lucky to have this wonderful, incredible family."

"You never have to get through anything without us," her father said, giving her a hug. "We're Callaways. All for one. One for all."

"Always, Dad." She ran to the door to meet the nurse who was coming to get her. She couldn't wait to see Max. She wouldn't feel completely better until he opened his eyes and smiled at her. Then her world would be right side up again.

* * *

As Emma left the room, Spencer ran a weary hand through his hair and looked at Hallie. "I guess that's it."

She gave him a warm smile. "I'm so glad you got good news."

"Thanks for staying with me."

"No problem. I learned a lot. I think I might even try my own hand at a stew."

He grinned at her teasing smile. "I told you I would bore you."

"You didn't. But I think I will find myself a cab and go home."

"Why don't I drive you?"

"You should stay with your mom."

He knew she was right, but he really didn't want to say goodbye to Hallie yet. He was just getting to know her, and he was afraid if he let her walk away now, he'd never see her again. The day's events had brought down her guard walls, but would they be back up in the morning? Would she get on a plane and fly off to her dream island and never come home again? "I'll walk you to the elevator then."

"Great."

The walk was far too short.

As she reached for the elevator button, he stepped in front of her. "Hallie…"

"What?"

"We need to get that drink."

"We will," she said.

"When you get back from the island?"

She shook her head. "I'm not going to the island."

"But the beach is calling, isn't it?"

"It was, until I spent half the night talking to you. You're very persuasive Spencer." She paused. "I'm going to give my dad a call in the morning and maybe go see him."

"Really?"

"You said some things that made sense."

"I'm glad. So if I'm that good, can I persuade you to give me your phone number now?"

She smiled. "I already did."

He gave her a questioning look. "What do you mean?"

"I put it in your phone when you went to the restroom earlier."

He grinned. "Sneaky."

"You really don't know anything about me."

"I'm looking forward to finding out more."

"I kind of feel the same way about you." She reached around him and pushed the button. "Before we say goodbye, I just need to know one thing."

"What's that?" he asked.

She stepped forward, put her hands on his head and pulled him into one hot and amazingly good kiss. Her lips were warm and inviting, and the spark that had been burning since he'd first laid eyes on her leapt into a full-blown flame. He felt a passion brewing that he hadn't felt in a very long time. He put his hands on her waist and held on, wanting to keep the kiss going for as long as possible.

Then the elevator dinged, and she broke away with a breathless smile. "Just as I thought," she said. "That mouth of yours is good for a lot more than talking."

He grinned. "Yours, too. That was hot. I'm going to call you tomorrow. You better answer."

Hallie stepped into the elevator. "I will," she said.

The elevator doors closed, and he walked back down the hall, feeling light on his feet and happier than he'd been in a decade.

The rest of his life was about to begin. He was closing the book on his past for good, and he was looking forward to a future—a future that was going to include one beautiful, gutsy redhead.

* * *

Emma sat by Max's side until dawn. The sun was just creeping through the slit in the curtains when Max began to stir. She got to her feet as his eyelids flickered and then slowly opened. She put her hand on his arm as he tried to focus. His skin was warm now, and it was so much better than the icy cold she'd felt the night before.

His gaze finally met hers.

"Max," she whispered.

His lips parted, but his voice was hoarse and rough when he said, "Emma."

"Don't try to talk," she said quickly. Seeing the confusion in his eyes, she added, "You're in the hospital. You were shot, but you're going to be all right." She gave him a smile, wanting to reassure him, wanting to take the sudden flash of fear out of his eyes. She suddenly realized where it was coming from. "Spencer is all right, too."

Relief moved across his face. He took several deeper

breaths and then said, "I'm sorry."

Her heart tore at his words. "You don't have anything to be sorry for."

"The wedding—"

"Will happen another day. Don't worry about it."

"All the money your parents spent—"

"Stop. It's going to be fine," she said firmly. "The only thing that matters is you. You're going to be all right. That's all I care about."

"You look so pretty."

She gave him a teary smile. "That's the drugs talking. I'm a mess."

"You have blood on your dress." He frowned. "How did you get blood on your clothes?"

"I hugged you," she said. "Right before they put you in the ambulance."

"How did I get out of the bank?"

"It's a long story. Spencer will tell you everything."

"Did anyone else get hurt?"

"You're the only one. Luckily there was a nurse in the bank. She helped Spencer take care of you."

"Did she have red hair?"

"She did."

"Spencer was hitting on her in line."

"I think he's still doing that," she said with a smile. "She spent half the night in the waiting room with him."

"Good for him."

"You should rest now." Her hand slid down his arm and she put her fingers around his.

He looked into her eyes. "Are you still going to marry me, Emma?"

"Try and stop me," she said. "Third time will be the charm. And I really don't care about any more wedding planning, Max. We can get married wherever. It's the marriage part I want, the having children and growing old together that's important. I want what my grandparents' have—the next sixty years with you."

"Only sixty?"

"Make that a hundred. Try to rest now."

"Kiss me first," he said.

She lowered her head and kissed him on the lips, infusing every bit of her love and passion for him in that one long kiss. "Sleep now."

"Now? After that?" he said. "I want another kiss."

"Tomorrow," she said with a laugh.

Despite his protest, his eyes were already drifting closed. She sat back down in the chair and then leaned back and closed her eyes, letting exhaustion sweep her into a happy dream of many more tomorrows with the man she loved.

Epilogue

Two weeks later – Christmas Eve

"I thought you were taking me out to dinner," Hallie said as Spencer ushered her up the steps of the San Francisco Courthouse.

He smiled. "You'll get dinner—eventually."

"That sounds ominous. What's going on?"

"It's a surprise."

Spencer had been surprising her a lot lately. In fact, they'd spent much of the last two weeks together. As promised, their first date had been to the Beachside Bar where he'd introduced her to San Francisco's finest rum drinks. They'd talked for hours over those drinks, and found they had more in common than just dark pasts.

She couldn't remember feeling so comfortable with a man so quickly, but going through a life and death situation with Spencer had vaulted them over the initial first date awkwardness, and their relationship was moving quickly past friendship into passion and maybe even love.

They'd both been through their own version of hell, but they were coming out of the darkness. Spencer had enrolled in a cooking class and was working on the weekends as a sous chef, and she'd just spoken to one of her former bosses at San Francisco General Hospital about working in the maternity ward. She thought bringing babies into the world would be a nice change of pace. She'd missed nursing, and it was time to stop running away from what she loved. Her punishment was over.

She'd never imagined a trip to the bank could turn her entire life upside down. And it wasn't just the robbery that had shaken her out of her stupor; it was Spencer.

After telling him her story, she'd been able to go back to her dad. Her father had apologized for not reacting the way she'd wanted. And she'd said she was sorry for not giving him a chance to react any way he wanted to. They'd made up and she'd found her dad to be far more understanding of what she'd gone through than she'd thought.

Speaking of her father…

"Don't forget, we have to get to my dad's house by eight," she said. "I promised I'd bring you by after dinner. He wants to meet the man who encouraged me to talk to him again."

"And I want to meet him. We'll be there in plenty of time." Spencer paused by the front door. "Before we go inside, I want to say something."

"What's that?" she asked, feeling a little nervous. It was a familiar feeling. In fact, she was starting to get used to the fluttery dance her stomach did every time Spencer was around. She was wildly attracted to the man; she just didn't know exactly what to do about it. After their fast start, they'd been taking things slow, but she'd been finding the pace a little slower than she wanted. In fact, she'd been taking a lot of cold showers lately.

Spencer gave her a serious look. "I want you, Hallie."

She swallowed hard, not sure what to say. "Okay."

He frowned. "Not exactly the reaction I was looking for."

"We're standing outside a courthouse."

"I know it's not the most romantic spot I could have picked, but I didn't want to go another minute without telling you how I feel. We've both been hurt by love. But I'm ready to take another chance—with you. If you're not ready yet, I'll wait. I know you loved Doug, and I want to respect that."

"How long will you wait?"

"As long as it takes for you to want me, too. I know I'm not the ideal man. I've got a prison record—"

"Hush," she said, putting her finger against his lips. "We've been all through that. I know what kind of man you are. I'm not afraid of your record or your past."

"Are you sure?"

"Positive. I already want you, Spencer. I'm scared of how much I want you. And after what we went through together, I don't want to waste any more time being afraid. I'd like to see where this relationship goes. So I'm in, all the way in." As she finished speaking, all her lingering doubts faded away. She was in love again. She'd never imagined she could be, but here she was.

"Thank God," Spencer said with heartfelt sincerity. "I feel the same way." He pulled her into his arms and kissed her.

"I'm glad you feel the same," she said breathlessly, but I hope you didn't bring me here to spring a surprise wedding on me."

"Well, someone is getting married, but it's not us. It's Emma and Max."

"Really? Here?"

"Emma didn't want to wait to put together another wedding. She wants to marry Max tonight."

"Isn't this family only?"

"You saved Max's life. Trust me, in Emma's eyes, you're already part of the family."

* * *

Emma glanced in the mirror of the ladies' restroom in the San Francisco Courthouse. Her sister, Nicole, met her gaze, and Emma smiled at their reflection, thinking back to the last time she'd gotten dressed for her wedding, her sister at her side. Then she'd worn a concoction of lace and silk. Now she had on a simple long-sleeve white dress with a sweetheart neckline perfect for showing off her grandmother's necklace.

"You look good," Nicole said.

"I think she could use a touch more eye-shadow," Shayla put in, as she came up behind them.

"Stop it. I look fine," Emma said with a smile, turning around to face them.

"Are you sure this is what you want?" Shayla asked, doubt in her eyes. "Maybe this is the wrong time to ask the question, but I know this isn't your dream wedding."

"My dream wedding is with the man I love, and he's waiting for me down the hall. I know he's here this time, because Sara checked for me. Nothing is going to go wrong today," she added with a little smile. "So let's get this show on the road."

"After you," Nicole said, waving her out of the bathroom.

Max and Spencer along with the Callaway men were waiting outside the judge's chambers. Max wore a dark gray suit and Emma's breath caught in her chest at the sight of him. He looked so handsome. But more importantly, he looked healthy and alive. He'd recovered quickly from his surgery, and neither one of them had wanted to wait another second to tie the knot.

"Ready to become Mrs. Max Harrison?" he asked, taking her hand.

She gave him a loving smile. "More than ready."

"Good. Let's do this so we can get to the honeymoon."

"We have the reception at my mom's house first."

"Don't remind me. I can't wait to get you alone, Emma Callaway."

"Soon to be Emma Callaway Harrison. I love you, Max. It's going to be me and you forever."

"Forever," he agreed, kissing her on the mouth.

"Hey, you two," Spencer said. "Save something for the ceremony."

She glanced over at Spencer, pleased to see the beautiful Hallie at his side. She had a feeling Spencer was going to get his happily-ever-after, too.

Max led her into the judge's chambers. And as they stood in front of the judge, promising to love each other forever, they were surrounded by their family and friends. There was love in every breath of air that she took, and Emma drank it all in. Their vows were more poignant now, knowing how close they'd come to losing each other and the dream of their lifetime.

"You may kiss the bride," the judge finally said.

Max gave her a look of love and said. "It's about damn time." And then his mouth covered hers.

THE END

Dear Reader:

I hope you enjoyed Max and Emma's wedding, and that you had a good time seeing Spencer and Hallie begin their love story. They'll be appearing in future Callaway books as well.

I have so many Callaway story ideas in my head that I thought it might be fun to do some novellas around big events in the family, stories that don't work for a full-length book but are great for a shorter length novella. I hope you'll enjoy the mix of long and shorter stories.

If you've missed any of the Callaway novels, here are the titles that are currently available: ON A NIGHT LIKE THIS (#1), SO THIS IS LOVE (#2), FALLING FOR A STRANGER (#3) and BETWEEN NOW AND FOREVER (#4). I've included summaries of these books following this letter.

My next full-length story, ALL A HEART NEEDS (Callaways #5) will be out in February of 2014 and features Sean and Jessica's story. You won't want to miss this one!

Happy Reading!

Barbara Freethy

THE CALLAWAY SERIES:
ON A NIGHT LIKE THIS (#1)

The second oldest of the Callaway clan, Aiden Callaway veered from the family tradition of urban firefighting and became a smokejumper, never questioning his choice until the job took the life of his friend, Kyle, and left Aiden with injuries and fractured memories. Everyone blames Aiden for what happened, but he doesn't remember, nor is he sure he wants to remember. The truth may clear Aiden of blame but destroy Kyle's reputation and hurt the people he left behind.

Aiden seeks help from an unlikely ally ...

Sara had always been untouchable, sweet, innocent, his sister's best friend, and the girl next door. But one reckless night in their youth took their relationship to a new level. Sara has never forgiven or forgotten the way Aiden brought it crashing down, but she's no longer that girl with the crazy crush. She's a woman in search of her own truth.

The sparks between Aiden and Sara have been smoldering for a very long time. Sara is afraid to take another chance on a man who broke her heart, and Aiden knows better than anyone how dangerous an intense fire can be.

As teenagers they weren't ready for each other. Are they ready now?

On A Night Like This (Callaways, #1) Available Now!

THE CALLAWAY SERIES:
SO THIS IS LOVE (#2)

Emma Callaway, a hot fire investigator clashes with Max Harrison, a cool homicide detective in SO THIS IS LOVE, the second book in the Callaway Series, by #1 NY Times Bestselling Author Barbara Freethy

For Max Harrison, love seduces and then destroys. His brother went to prison for love. His father left his family for love. And Max is determined not to follow in their footsteps, until he meets Emma...

Emma runs into burning buildings without an ounce of fear and embraces life as if every day is a new adventure. But while she's fearless on the job, Emma is a coward when it comes to love. Betrayed by an ex-boyfriend, Emma has no intention of putting her heart on the line again, until she meets Max...

As the fires around the city rage, the heat between them ignites in a blaze of passion that's far more dangerous. Will it destroy them or will they finally get everything they ever wanted...

So This Is Love (Callaways, #2) Available Now!

THE CALLAWAY SERIES: FALLING FOR A STRANGER (#3)

Ria is as sexy and sultry as a warm tropical night and as beautifully dangerous as the island drinks she serves at the beachside bar on Isla de los Suenos -- The Island of Dreams. But Ria is not as carefree as she appears, and the pretense is wearing her down. One night she risks everything to escape from reality.

Drew Callaway is a former Navy pilot and rescue operative looking for his own escape from a life that has seen too much tragedy. Meeting Ria is like embracing the sun, and their single night together is life-changing. But the dream quickly fades when Ria is killed in a tragic accident at sea.

Months later, thousands of miles away from where they first met, Drew sees a woman who looks just like Ria. She claims her name is Tory, and that they've never met before, but he can see that she's in trouble, and he can't walk away. He's going to save her whether she wants it or not.

Drew isn't afraid of a little danger, but can he risk losing his heart to a beautiful stranger?

Falling For A Stranger (Callaways, #3) Available Now!

THE CALLAWAY SERIES:
BETWEEN NOW AND FOREVER (#4)

Nicole met Ryan when he was a handsome, cocky teenager with a desire to fly high above the clouds. Ryan encouraged Nicole to dream big and promised her a lifetime of happiness, but several years into their lives together, they were faced with obstacles bigger than either had ever imagined. Their love faltered. They lost their way and considered what had once been unthinkable—the end of their forever.

But now fate throws them a curve, an event that forces them back together, that strips their emotions bare and is both terrifying and strangely unifying. For the first time in a long while they have to face each other, and not only talk but also listen, because their lives depend on it—not only their lives, but also the life of their six-year-old son.

Secrets and lies frame a perilous journey to the truth that takes Nicole and Ryan to Angel's Bay, a place where miracles sometimes happen. But in order to get that miracle, Nicole and Ryan must work together and learn how to trust and love each other again. Only then will they be able to save their family and find their way to happily ever after.

Between Now And Forever (Callaways, #4) Available Now!

Book List

About The Author

Barbara Freethy is a #1 New York Times Bestselling Author of 35 novels ranging from contemporary romance to romantic suspense and women's fiction. Traditionally published for many years, Barbara turned to Indie publishing in 2011 and in two years has sold over 3 million ebooks! Fourteen of her titles have appeared on the New York Times and USA Today Bestseller Lists.

Known for her emotional and compelling stories of love, family, mystery and romance, Barbara enjoys writing about ordinary people caught up in extraordinary adventures. She is currently writing a connected family series, The Callaways, which includes: ON A NIGHT LIKE THIS (#1), SO THIS IS LOVE (#2), FALLING FOR A STRANGER (#3) and BETWEEN NOW AND FOREVER (#4). There will be at least eight books in the Callaway series, and if you love series with romance, suspense and a little adventure, you'll love the Callaways.

Barbara also recently released the WISH SERIES, a series of books connected by the theme of wishes including: A SECRET WISH (#1), JUST A WISH AWAY (#2) and WHEN WISHES COLLIDE (#3).

Other popular standalone titles include: DON'T SAY A WORD, SILENT RUN and RYAN'S RETURN.

Barbara's books have won numerous awards - she is a six-time finalist for the RITA for best contemporary romance from Romance Writers of America and a two-time winner for DANIEL'S GIFT and THE WAY BACK HOME.

Barbara has lived all over the state of California and currently resides in Northern California where she draws much of her inspiration from the beautiful bay area.

For a complete listing of books, as well as excerpts and contests, and to connect with Barbara:

Visit Barbara's Website: www.barbarafreethy.com
Join Barbara on Facebook: www.facebook.com/barbarafreethybooks
Follow Barbara on Twitter: www.twitter.com/barbarafreethy

CPSIA information can be obtained at www.ICGtesting.com
Printed in the USA
LVOW12s1935010714

392552LV00030B/1468/P